D1095856

DATE DUE

*She and the
Dubious Three*

She and the Dubious Three

Dorothy Crayder

Illustrated by Velma Ilsley

Atheneum 1974 New York

Library of Congress Cataloging in Publication Data

Crayder, Dorothy.
  She and the dubious three.

  SUMMARY: Maggie discovers that adventure can
lead to near disaster as well as to opportunity when
she investigates a young hippie couple to see if they
have kidnapped the child they claim is theirs.
  [1. Mystery and detective stories. 2. Venice—
Fiction] I. Ilsley, Velma, illus. II. Title.
PZ7.C8597Sf   [Fic]   74-75559
ISBN 0-689-30407-2

". . . an unlesson'd girl, unschool'd, unpractis'd;
Happy in this, she is not yet so old
But she may learn. . . ."

Merchant of Venice
Act III Sc. II

She and the
Dubious Three

1

Maggie thought it was all most peculiar.

To begin with, why did these hippies hate her so much?

All she had done was say "Hello" to their hippie baby. It had seemed like a normal, friendly remark to make to a fellow traveler sitting eyeball-to-eyeball with you.

The baby hadn't minded. The baby had loved her. It had taken its mangled hunk of bread out of its mouth and offered it to her with a grubby, little hand. And it had given her a big loving smile.

The hippie parents had not smiled. The mother

had tried to turn the baby to the window. But the baby was not interested in the empty platform of a railway station. It was interested in Maggie. It was wriggling and shoving to get off its mother's lap.

Maggie wanted to let them know that she'd like to play with their baby, but there was something forbidding about the hippies. Behind their dark glasses, they were a dusty blur of unknown origin.

They began to whisper to each other, and the father stood up. The compartment was tiny, and the space between the two facing banks of seats was narrow. He climbed over their guitar, which occupied the seat next to him, stepped gingerly over the legs of two nuns who were sitting on Maggie's side, and went out the glass door. As he disappeared down the corridor of the car, the baby stared after him, its face puckered with concern.

"Daddy will be back," the mother said.

So these hippies were American. This made it all the more peculiar. You would think, Maggie thought, that fellow Americans meeting on an Italian train would at least greet each other with questions like, "Hi there, where you from?" and "Where you going?" and "Who do you think's going to win the pennant this year?" Stuff like that.

Maybe they hated her because she was wearing square drip-dries instead of jeans. Maybe they thought she was a rich Establishment kid who would brainwash their child. If so, that would be a big laugh, because her father was only an English teacher and it was her great-aunt Yvonne who was treating her to this expensive, educational trip to Italy and she wasn't crazy about the drip-dries either.

The baby's eyes were fixed on the corridor, and its face remained puckered.

It was a cute baby, dirty but cute. Maggie had never seen a hippie baby before. In Tilton, Iowa, where she came from, she thought there might be some law against them. In Tilton, too, you usually knew whether babies were boys or girls, but behind all the smudge and raggedy jeans, you couldn't tell about this one.

Not even by its hair. This was another thing that was peculiar. Its parents' hair, tied back with Indian headbands, was long, ratty, and hippie-ish. But the baby's was shortish and squeaky clean, just like all the straight babies' hair she'd ever known.

Before Maggie had time to ponder over this peculiarity, the father returned. He shook his head, and after he had climbed his way back and sat down, she heard him whisper, "We'll have to stay here."

The mother's reply was inaudible, but her mouth set grimly.

Have to? Why did they want to move? Not be-

of little old, harmless her, for goodness' sake?
didn't make sense. Unless it was because no
had told her she had morning breath or that
she was suddenly sending out bad vibes. Whatever
the reason, this funny business did make her feel
unpopular and awkward.

"Mike, Mike . . ." the baby was saying to its
father, peering at him, its face no longer puckered
. . . but bewildered?

Mike? Why not *Daddy?* If the baby was bewildered, so was she. Why does the mother say
"Daddy," and the baby say "Mike"?

Surreptitiously, Maggie studied the threesome
across the way from her. That baby did not look
like its father. And not all that much like its mother.
What if these hippies were not this baby's parents?
What if . . .

Whoa there! Maggie cautioned herself. The love
of adventure has just gotten into your blood. Do
not let it go to your head. Do not let your imagination run wild. Do not forget that you are someone
who had to be She, the Adventuress to give you
the courage to make a trip like this *all alone by
ship.* Do not forget that it is okay for a beginner
like you to be ready for adventure, but do not be
too ready. Do not be dumb.

With some difficulty, Maggie pulled her eyes
away from the hippies and turned to the nuns. Sep-

arated from her by one seat, these two figures, draped in strange, purple habits, their faces completely screened off by huge shovellike coifs, sat still and silent.

Indeed, the silence in the compartment had become oppressive and spooky. Somehow all the more spooky for knowing that outside, in the city of Genoa, there was plenty of noise—nice, friendly Italian noise.

The spookiness set off an urgent need to know that this train was *positively* going to Venice. The ticket, which she was clutching in a hand now beginning to sweat, was stamped *Venezia*, Italian for Venice. All that proved was that she had the right ticket. Along with her newly acquired taste for adventure, Maggie had also become newly brave about traveling all by herself on a foreign train in a foreign country. But there was no sense in letting bravery keep you on the wrong train, was there?

The two silent, purple figures did not exactly invite dumb questions from strange kids. And what if the nuns hated her, too?

The thought of being on the wrong train made Maggie risk their displeasure. She stretched out across the seat separating her from the nuns and peered under a coif.

"Excuse me, please . . ." Maggie said, timidly. The nun's startled face broke into a smile. The

7

other nun smiled, too. They both had plump and jolly faces. Maggie smiled back. They understood smiles. But what else?

"Excuse me, but this *is* the train for Venice, isn't it?"

The nuns did not understand English. They continued to smile and, their coifs bobbing, they spoke in a foreign language. It wasn't Italian, so the phrase book Maggie had with her wouldn't help.

The hippie father spoke: "Yes," he said.

Maggie pulled herself back and straightened up. "Oh, thank you very much. I'm glad, because that's where I'm supposed to go."

The hippie father almost smiled. The hippie mother remained grim. It may have been her imagination again, but the funny look the hippie mother gave the hippie father said: "I will kill you if you get friendly with this girl."

The hippie baby made another attempt to get to Maggie, but it was a feeble attempt because it was becoming drowsy.

Presently, a soft hum took Maggie's mind off the hippies. The locomotive was warming up, and any second now this beautiful continental train would be starting and She, a brave Adventuress, would be on her way through a strange and beautiful country.

The hum of the locomotive increased, and then

there were shouts of *"Tutti in carrozza! Tutti in carrozza!"*

All aboard! This was it!

Maggie caught her breath and looked out the window. Now, there *was* something to see. A conductor was beckoning wildly. Then a man came running down the platform, running with a long, steady lope. As she heard the locomotive revving up, she pressed closer to the window to see if the man would make it. But the train started to move, and she lost sight of him.

The movement of the train had different effects on the nuns and on the baby. The nuns opened a bag and brought out bread, salami, and tomatoes and began to eat; the baby fell asleep, still clutching its bread.

The salami smelled strong. Salami being eaten at nine o'clock in the morning smelled strongly foreign, a good smell for the beginning of an adventure.

Maggie sank back in the plush seat. If there was to be a new adventure, it was now in the hands of fate (and the engineer of this train) and what was going to be was going to be. It was lovely and relaxing to turn yourself over to fate.

Maggie shared her seat with an enormous bag. It was only because she was so skinny that this was possible. The bag had been Maggie's going away present to herself, and for ten days and eleven nights, traveling by plane to New York and by ship to Genoa, Italy, she and the bag had never once been separated from each other. Somewhere in it there was a map of Italy. In order to find that, she had to rummage around family portraits, beauty aids, guidebooks, a mystery, bubble gum, a diary, and various other objects besides her passport and traveler's checks and Italian money called lire, which she was going to have to bone up on. Many people had wondered how such a skinny girl could carry such a load on her shoulder. Her mother, who was an imaginative worrier, had worried about the bag making her permanently lopsided. So far this had not happened.

She found the map. Her social science teacher, Mrs. North, had given it to her with a string attached to it. "Maggie," Mrs. North had said, "please *use* this map. I sincerely hope this expensive trip pays off by improving your geography." Mrs. North was a pain-in-the-neck.

But being treated to an expensive and educational trip was a big responsibility. Half the population of Tilton was either counting on her to be educated by this trip or to be taking it for their personal benefit. She had been asked to eat, see, and do for half the town—everything from getting a

recipe for spaghetti to having an audience with the pope.

Maggie began to struggle with the map. It was a large map, which had been folded across its width and length many times to reduce it to pocket size. In the close quarters of the compartment, with nothing to rest it on, it became a gigantic puzzle of folds that refused to be folded. Maggie was trying to fold it down to the part that ran across the top of the boot from Genoa to Venice. Maggie and inanimate objects were old enemies: for her, rubber bands broke, staplers refused to staple, glue ran all over the place and forever joined together things meant to remain separate. And always during these battles, her tongue stuck out. Watching this battle were the nuns, who were now deep into salami and tomatoes, the hippie mother with the hippie baby asleep in her lap, and the hippie father.

The hippie father leaned forward with the obvious intention of coming to Maggie's assistance (regardless of what his old woman might think of this courtesy), when the door to the compartment opened and the man who had been running for the train appeared.

The nuns kept on eating. The baby kept on sleeping.

But the hippie father froze. And so did the hippie mother.

The man gave the compartment a quick once over. There were two empty seats: one next to the guitar and the one between Maggie and the nuns. The man chose the seat next to Maggie. With Maggie's map spread out, it would have seemed more natural to take the seat next to the guitar.

The hippie father leaned back, and Maggie pulled the map to one side to make room for the man.

The man placed his black Homburg hat and dispatch case on the rack overhead. He carried no other luggage, only a newspaper.

While the man's back was to them, Maggie caught the hippies raising their eyebrows at each other.

Since this man with his Homburg, his short hair, his ultraconservative blue suit, and his dispatch case was Mr. Establishment himself, Maggie was not surprised at the hippies' reaction.

The man sat down and gave Maggie and her map, which now covered her from her toes to the tip of her nose, a sallow, conservative smile. Then, as she began to struggle again, he said, in English with a faint accent:

"The help, yes?"

"*Grazie.*" (Using what little Italian she knew in an emergency, was a habit Maggie was trying to cultivate.)

"I speak English."

"Oh. Then, yes please."

"What it is you wish to accomplish?"

Maggie explained.

Swiftly, expertly, he undid Maggie's mistakes and folded the map properly.

"There you are," he said to her. And to the hippies: "Your little daughter, she is the guide?"

Maggie repressed a giggle. This man must be crazy. It was out of respect for Aunt Yvonne, whom she had never met, that she had not worn jeans while traveling on the train and was disgustingly neat and tidy in her drip-dries.

The hippies were astonished.

"*Man* . . ." The hippie father implied that he,

too, thought the man was crazy.

The man's eyes swept over the compartment, brushed past the nuns, and came back to Maggie.

"I'm nobody's daughter," Maggie said.

It was the man's turn to raise an eyebrow.

"You are an—?" he asked.

The temptation was almost irresistible to pretend that she was an orphan and an only child. But in one fell swoop to kill off her mother and her father who, as parents went, were pretty great and little old Sam, her kid brother? Not even him, now that distance was making him surprisingly lovable.

So, Maggie said: "I mean I'm nobody's daughter here. I'm traveling alone."

"Alone? From where?"

"Tilton, Iowa, U.S.A."

The man gave Maggie a look that was sharply penetrating as well as skeptical.

"It is all by yourself that you are doing this?"

It could be a breakthrough for downtrodden kids all over the world who are subject to personal questions from total strangers if, just for once, she were to answer: "No, sir. And not only is your question rude, but, sir, you have just sat down on my slightly invisible traveling companion and squashed him. Or her." That would get a *rise* out of him, she bet. Ha! Ha! Ha!

But no—enter meek Maggie! For the millionth

time, she explained about Aunt Yvonne treating her to the trip, about how she had flown to New York and traveled by ship all by herself, and about how she was now traveling all the way to Cortina d'Ampezzo, Italy, still alone. She was alone because Aunt Yvonne, who was supposed to meet her in Genoa, had had an accident. But, in Venice some lovely friends of her aunt would meet her and put her on the bus that would positively take her to Cortina.

With the last breath she had left from this long recital, Maggie said: "I certainly hope they do meet me."

"And I have the same hope," the man said. "From out of Venice there are many buses."

That, Maggie thought, was a very sinister remark to make to a stranger in need of reassurance.

"Oh, someone will meet me. Either the Rossettis or a substitute," she replied with bravado.

"Myself, I get off at Milan, but—" the man glanced at the hippies. "Are you by the chance—?"

The hippies both stiffened.

"Please don't worry about me. My aunt was hysterical over my making this trip alone, so I'll be met—"

But the Establishment was not about to let these hippies off the hook. He talked right over Maggie.

"So it is not Venice you go to?"

It was because Maggie didn't like the way the Establishment was prodding the hippies that she dropped her eyes. And that's why she saw the slight movement the hippie mother's elbow made as it dug into the hippie father. The dig was not her imagination. This dig looked like a warning nudge to her.

"No," the hippie father said.

"Trieste," the hippie mother said.

The hippie father fiddled with the raggedy edge of his jeans.

"Trieste? Ah, but then it is Venice you *do* go to in order to get to Trieste?"

One point for the Establishment, the hippies acknowledged with sulky nods.

"*Through* it," the mother added.

"Without to have a look at Venice, not one look?"

Disbelief and displeasure were in equal parts. That's hippies for you, he implied, no respect for famous cities either.

"Man, Venice is strictly for tourists," the hippie father jabbed back in American hippie English.

"But of course." The man smiled condescendingly. "It always was, from the beginning."

Two points for the Establishment?

The hippie father reached into his shoulder bag and took out a paperback. Maggie could see that it was about Zen. He studied the cover, first the front, then the back, reading the blurbs with curiously in-

16

tense concentration. The hippie mother bit her lip and looked out the window. The nuns cut some more thick slabs off their salamis. The man opened his newspaper. It was an Italian paper. The baby still slept, still clutched the bread.

And Maggie remembered that she was supposed to look out the window and see Italy because that's what this trip was all about: educational.

Looking out the window, she saw a mountain, practically flattening her nose. Turning her head the other way, she looked through the glass separating the compartment from the corridor and out another window, one running the length of the corridor. Out there she could see the harbor and the masts of ships. Sea or mountain? Which should it be? To get a good view of the sea, she would have to climb over the hippies, the Establishment, the nuns, and the guitar. For the moment, the mountain won.

Then, without any warning, the mountain disappeared as they entered a tunnel.

Sitting in the blackness with a bunch of strangers, with Italy having disappeared, and the smell of salami stronger than ever, another smell entered the compartment: the fishy smell of suspicion.

Why had the hippie mother nudged the hippie father?

2

Unfortunately, from an educational point of view, it was people who interested Maggie more than places. Not that the Italy that streamed behind her like a scenic ribbon wasn't pretty and interestingly foreign, with mountains that her map said were the Appenines, and vineyards, rice fields, poplars, cedars, and also bell towers, which the Establishment said were called *campaniles*. And once in a while there was a castle in the distance where a real princess might be living.

But the scenery wasn't peculiar, and the hippies were.

When Mrs. North said, "Maggie will now give the class a description of the topography of Italy as seen from a rapidly moving train," she would most likely say, "The hippie father's beard wasn't very old and the hippie mother never did take the price tag off her dirty old jeans and the baby seemed to be sleeping an awfully long time."

The nuns didn't stop eating, and she herself was beginning to starve to death with the garlicky smell of salami tantalizing her.

All the people who had helped to get her on this train—the ship's stewardess, the porters, the taxi driver, the conductor—had forgotten to tell her what to do about eating. A skimpy breakfast on the ship at seven in the morning, skimpy because of excitement, was not going to last until she got to Cortina late in the afternoon. Once or twice she and her best friend, Diane, had tried unsuccessfully to faint; interesting as fainting might be, she didn't want it to happen while traveling alone in Italy.

"Please, how do you get to eat on this train?" Maggie asked the Establishment.

The Establishment suggested that she buy a box lunch, *un cestino*, when they got to Milan.

"It is most often good—perhaps cold chicken, bread, fruit, and the little carafe of wine, and it will cost only about a thousand lire."

"A *thousand*—?"

"It is only a dollar and sixty at today's exchange."

"*Only?* for lunch?"

Maggie decided this was the time to let the hippies know they didn't have to hate her for being rich.

"At home, I never spend more than seventy-five cents for lunch. Never." Then, loud and clear and with a note of pride! "Because in our family most of the time we are busted."

"But it is your Aunt Yvonne . . ."

"Who is treating me. That's true. But not to everything."

Aunt Yvonne's name recalled the warning that Maggie was not to get off the train for any reason at all, which must include starvation.

"They'll come with the boxes," the Establishment assured her.

From then on until they got to Milan, floating dreamlike over the Italian landscape—and over the hippies too—was a breast of cold chicken, which was Maggie's favorite part.

When they pulled into the big glass-enclosed station of Milan, the Establishment collected his hat and dispatch case.

"Now, *signorina*—" he said to Maggie, in a tone not calculated to reassure her, "if by the mischance the people they fail to meet you, your little phrase book it should get you to the bus. Venetians, *they* are kind." Pointedly, his eyes flicked coldly over the hippies. "*Arrivederla.*"

That was the formal goodbye to strangers.

"*Ciao,*" Maggie replied for the benefit of the hippies. That was the casual, hip goodbye of friends and young people.

The way the hippies slumped in their seats and let themselves go, it was easy to see they were glad to be rid of the Establishment.

Maggie watched the Establishment stride off. He became just another one of an army of men all with dispatch cases, in business suits. Milan must be where the Establishment was invented. Maggie saw him brush past a burly, shorter replica of himself, and they appeared to exchange apologies.

A vendor did come into the train with the box lunches. Maggie had used lire to pay for her taxi, porters, and for her railroad ticket, but as she had been handed from one to the other, the information had been passed that she needed help. Now she was on her own. She extracted a fistful of lire and held them out.

For the first time, the hippie mother spoke out loud: in Italian to the vendor. Then she reached over and plucked the required lire from Maggie's hand and gave it to the vendor.

"Oh," Maggie said. "Thank you."

The hippie mother merely nodded. She bought

two boxes for them, too.

"The man told it like it was," the hippie father said.

And he had: there was a nice plump piece of chicken, bread and butter, grapes, and the carafe of wine. It looked delicious. Peering into Maggie's box inquisitively, the nuns thought so, too. As for the wine, Maggie thought that to drink it at lunch would be the most sophisticated act of her life so far. Not that she ever drank it any other time either, except a sip once in a long time when her parents were having a celebration.

With the arrival of the boxes, the baby woke up and grabbed for a chicken leg. The hippies both smiled at the baby. The baby smiled back and held out its arms to the father.

Maggie was herself eating the breast of chicken, thinking it to be the most fantastic she had ever had.

"Hi, Charlie—man," Mike said.

Charlie beamed at Mike.

So at least that mystery was cleared up: it was a boy.

"Hi, Charlie," the mother said, nice and friendly.

But the baby shook its head. Indeed, it stared at the mother as if she were a total stranger.

"Like, Charlie, what's the matter?" the mother asked anxiously.

Charlie continued to shake his head. And stretched

out his arms to Mike.

"Like you know I don't dig this—" the mother seemed more embarrassed than anxious as she handed Charlie to Mike.

"Neither do I," Maggie thought. "It's getting more and more peculiar."

"Like say 'hi' to Vicky—" Mike coaxed.

But Charlie had lost interest in Mike and turned toward Maggie. She just naturally smiled, and Charlie reached toward her with a fat, grubby arm. This time it was Mike who turned him away. This time, however, Charlie arched his back and pulled his mouth down and began to get purple. Vicky quickly shoved a chicken leg in his face; it worked. Charlie forgot Maggie and grabbed for it. Vicky and Mike sighed with relief.

Once again, Maggie was puzzled. All the parents she had ever known were delighted to dump their kids on willing bystanders. Of course they had not been hippie parents. Parents? Once again, the question what if . . . reared itself?

And Maggie felt a shiver of excitement. To be honest about it, she had to admit it was a lovely shiver.

Then Maggie gave her attention to the wine. She took a tentative sip and waited for something interesting to happen to her. Drinking it made her feel a little like Barbra Streisand, who was high up on the list of people she took turns pretending to be. She wondered what her mother would think of her guzzling wine all by herself in the middle of the day with nothing to celebrate but a possible adventure. Actually, she didn't have to wonder, she knew: her mother would think that one glass of wine would stunt her growth, make her drunk, and turn her into a wine addict. Or that it would clog her pores. Her mother was always worrying about her pores. So far her pores were one of her best features. The other one was her smile.

As to the taste of the wine, it wasn't as good as a Coke, but it was better than water.

The train had just begun to roll again when the door opened and a man came in. There was something familiar about him. Where had she seen him? Then Maggie remembered. He was the short, stocky man the Establishment had bumped into.

This time the hippies were too busy eating and feeding Charlie to pay much attention. The man took the seat next to the guitar. He opened his dispatch case, took out a Simenon mystery, and dug into it.

With the second glass of wine and the gentle rocking of the train, Barbra Streisand departed and Maggie began to get sleepy. She struggled to keep her eyes open: she knew she owed it to Aunt Yvonne, Mrs. North, and all those other people to stay awake.

Then, too, she wanted to keep her eyes on these peculiar hippies. But most importantly she was afraid of not being awake in time to get off at Venice. There was nothing for it but to ask the hippies to please wake her up. However, they too were settling in for a nap. And the nuns had finally eaten themselves into a stupor and were now snoring gently and in counterpoint. This left Charlie and the man. Charlie was now wide awake and banging the chicken leg on the window; the man was absorbed in his Simenon. Maggie climbed over the hippies' and the nuns' legs and whispered to the man, whose Simenon was in Italian, but who might be made to understand:

"*Scusi, signor—*"

25

The man lifted his eyes slowly from the book. They were not friendly eyes.

"Uh—" Maggie began.

"You wish to know where is the toilet?"

He was not a man who hemmed and hawed.

"No, thank you. I wish to be awakened in Venice, please."

"Yes."

Maggie climbed back over the legs. When she sat down, she wondered why the man had taken it for granted that English was her language. After all, made in the U.S.A. wasn't stamped *all* over her face, was it?

Peculiar.

Maggie didn't fall sound asleep. She knew better than to trust a man who was deep into a mystery to wake her. Herself, when she was caught up in a bunch of clues, the house could burn down and she wouldn't know it. Or so her mother said. Besides, this man's eyes were definitely unfriendly.

So she just dozed for a while with one eye open, so to speak, the way her dog, Boy, did when a cat was in the neighborhood.

By the time they reached *Lago di Garda*, Maggie was wide awake. She joined the nuns at the corridor window to get a glimpse of the lake. The impression was one of clear blue water resting coolly and quietly at the foot of mountains feathered with woods. She hoped Cortina was going to have a lake like that.

The man came out of the compartment and, taking a place at the window, lit a cigarette.

Maggie went back in. The hippies were whispering away for all they were worth, their heads close together. They stopped when Maggie came in.

On the one hand, this embarrassed her, as if she ought to say, "Excuse me for living." On the other hand, she became more suspicious.

Feeling so unpopular with the hippies made Maggie miss everyone who had ever loved her—or merely liked her—or had just been lukewarm. In particular, she missed all the nice, warm, friendly people who had been her shipboard companions and from whom she had parted only a few hours ago. She missed an old lady named Mrs. Stone, who had been her cabinmate, but she specially missed a boy named Jasper, who was at this moment flying home to the United States. She and Jasper had promised to write to each other and Maggie felt this was a good time to keep that promise.

She took out her pad of air mail stationery and her ballpoint pen and wrote a letter that began with salami:

If this letter smells of salami do not blame it on me, but on some nuns. They have been eating it all the way from Genoa, which is miles of salami. Fantastic.

Then it went on to tell about the peculiar hippies and their fantastic hippie baby. And ended with "*Ciao*, your friend, *Maggie*."
Or almost ended there.
The first P.S. said:

This train just went past *Verona!* Holy Cow! Romeo and Juliet! Travel is absolutely fantastic.

Then came

P.P.S. I am getting tired of the word fantastic, aren't you? If you can invent a new word for it, send it to me by return mail. Please. It could make you famous.

And finally,

P.P.P.S. The hippie baby is now playing with a crazy bunch of sticks, which is probably a hippie-type toy that can poke its eyes out. I do not think true blue genuine parents would allow this. I know mine wouldn't. I think there is some very funny business going on, and I am getting more and more suspicious.

Along with Jasper's address, Maggie wrote in block letters: FLY IT, and then in case the Italians didn't understand that, underneath she wrote: VIA AEREA.

In fact, it was the nuns who alerted Maggie when they approached Venice. Awakening, mysteriously at the same instant, it was they who spotted the beginning of the lagoon. With coifs bobbing excitedly, they gestured to Maggie to join them at the corridor window.

As the train began its trip over the causeway that linked the mainland to Venice, the corridor became crowded with sightseers jabbering in various languages. Even the hippies were there. However, not the man with the Simenon. He was more interested in finding out who did it, which Maggie for one could understand.

It was sad that a body of water with such a pretty name as lagoon could be so icky—all muddy and oil slicked. But that made it all the more amazing that rising from it in the distance was the "Pearl of the Adriatic"—*Venice!*

The nuns' coifs rocked from side to side very much like bells. Other people settled for oohing and ahing in their native tongues.

As they sped toward Venice, Maggie's pulse quickened. But truthfully, not because she was about to enter this watery dream of a city, but because she hoped to make her safe—and correct—exit from it.

What if no one was there to meet her? What if there were another girl on the train with long, straight black hair that was naturally wavy but was straightened with rollers, carrying an enormous bag, wearing a blue drip-dry dress, and who was traveling all alone? Accidents will certainly happen as she well knew.

Thoughts like these sent her hurriedly to her phrase book and "When You Travel by Bus or Taxi." The best she could find for her purpose was "*Voglio andare al Corso Garibaldi*," which meant "I wish to go to *Corso* Garibaldi." But she didn't wish to go there at all. She wished with all her might to go to Cortina d'Ampezzo. Okay. If she kept her cool, she could remember that. It also helped that the word for bus in Italian was easy to remember: it was *autobus*. And, of course, she would never forget that "*Aiuto! Polizia!*" was Italian for "Help! Police!"

When she stood on the seat to get her suitcase down from the rack, the hippie father helped her, which was a nice surprise.

"Oh, thank you and . . . *ciao*." Maggie smiled

at the three hippies.

"*Ciao* . . ." the father responded, sort of raising a fist.

The mother looked at him with what seemed to be amused surprise. Then she broke down and said, "*Ciao*." Now that they were parting?

"Chow, chow, chow," Charlie said, delighted with its sound and himself.

For one second his grubby, sticky little hand was in Maggie's. It made her feel awfully like holding a tiny bird—tender and responsible. She squeezed it gently and let it go. Reluctantly.

She waggled some fingers at the nuns, and they bobbed their coifs at her.

The Simenon man stood up, but kept right on reading as he did so.

Out on the platform, with people streaming past her, Maggie stood still. She watched the nuns glide off in one direction and the hippies, with the Simenon man not too far behind them, shuffle off in another. Not a soul came toward her. Not a soul paid any attention to her. For all she knew she had become invisible.

Do not panic! That was the voice of someone who had never been all alone at her age in a foreign place having to get to another foreign place without being able to speak the foreign language.

How long could she stay there and wait without

missing the bus? Voice or no voice, this question made her panic. When she panicked she usually got sick to her stomach first and then cried. Her mother said she turned the color of botulism, if it had any color. (Which it doesn't, her father said.)

Her stomach had just begun to feel awful when the woman came up to her.

"You'd better be Maggie—"

Never before had Maggie been so happy to accommodate anyone.

"Oh, I am, I am—"

"That's a relief. She couldn't remember whether you said blue or pink, so I looked for green. I'm Agnes Grant."

Agnes Grant cawed like a crow and looked like a big bulldog, bowlegs and all. She was not cuddly, but she was as familiar as corn and apple pie: she was from someplace back home.

"Are you going to put me on the bus to Cortina —please?"

That was meant to be a rhetorical question. The answer, therefore, came as a shock.

"Nope."

Maggie had picked up her suitcase, which heavy. She put it down.

"Nope, I'm not. And for a good reason." Agnes Grant paused ominously.

"Why?" Maggie asked, choking on the word.

"Because you're not going to Cortina."

"But, I *am* too!" Panic was definitely coming back.

"Oh, no you're not." Agnes Grant was being coy. This was weirdly unbecoming and frightening.

This Agnes Grant was anything but "lovely," and Maggie hated her. If Agnes Grant was Aunt Yvonne's idea of lovely, what was Aunt Yvonne herself going to be like? But maybe this Agnes Grant was an impostor?

"Are—are you teasing?" Maggie asked, stalling for time while she tried to collect her wits, which were in splinters.

"Anything but—as you will find out. She said I should break it to you gently. Okay! Here goes! You're staying in Venice."

"With *you?*"

"Lord, no. With her. I'm only passing through. She's staying here in Venice."

Maggie thought it was high time she tested this Agnes Grant.

"Who's *she?*" she asked.

"Who's she? Who do you think she is for pete's sake?"

"My aunt," Maggie said lamely.

"None other. Come along now, we'd better get cracking—"

Agnes Grant picked up the suitcase as if it were a feather.

"But Cortina—"

Agnes Grant was already charging down the platform.

"She'll tell you about it. I'm not supposed to."

Maggie followed her. After all, this woman did have her suitcase. And after all, just because she'd suddenly gotten to like adventure didn't mean she had suddenly turned into a lady wrestler, did it? And after all, underneath she was still little old, mushy Maggie, wasn't she?

For all I know, Maggie thought, I am now being kidnapped, and I should be yelling "*Aiuto! Polizia!*" at the top of my lungs instead of following this woman like a spineless moron. The question is: Why am I doing this? The answer is: Because Agnes Grant is from the Midwest like me so she can't be all bad. If she were foreign, I would be yelling my head off, which only shows how dangerous patriotism can be when carried to extremes. Besides, I'm not rich enough to be kidnapped. But . . . is Aunt Yvonne?

Maggie had been so busy analyzing and interviewing herself she hadn't noticed where she was going. It came, therefore, as a great surprise to find herself walking down some steps leading right to *water*.

"Gosh!"

Agnes Grant laughed.

"Never saw anything like this before, did you?"

Maggie blinked. No, she never had seen anything like this before. But then who had if they had never been to Venice?

A motorboat slid up to the landing stage at the bottom of the steps.

"Here's our taxi. It's called a *motoscafo* and costs a pot I'm here to tell you. The *vaporetto*—the water-bus over there—wasn't fancy enough—"

In a stupor, Maggie rolled her eyes toward the *vaporetto*. Mingling with the crowd boarding it, she spotted the hippies. Did that water-bus go to Trieste? Somehow, she didn't think so.

Peculiar.

Both she and Charlie were being kidnapped.

Without a murmur from either one of them.

3

It was all shimmering sunlight, watery shadows, and lacy palaces, red and pale gold palaces floating up from the sea.

Maggie stood on the open deck of the *motoscafo* as it scudded over the canal and did not listen to Agnes Grant cawing names and places and facts and figures; particularly, she did not listen to the news that, "All this is sinking at the rate of a couple of inches a century. Someone didn't use his head."

"The Grand Canal, the main drag—"

Candy-striped mooring poles and black gondolas, sleek and shiny and fitted out with rugs and flowers, and gondoliers in straw hats with red ribbons; and instead of trucks, barges carrying crates, vegetables, and Coca-Cola.

"People where fish should be—"

Shimmering, shimmering, shimmering.

And little canals where streets should be.

And her father had been right: when ice cream, hair, peanut butter sandwiches, and millions of other objects, ideas, people, and places had all been fantastic, what was the word for this place?

"The Rialto—"

And there it was, looking like itself in pictures— little shops strung together in a hump over the canal.

"The *Campanile* of Saint Mark—the domes of the Basilica—"

Maggie was sure she imagined that bells were ringing from both sides of the canal.

This must be what beautiful was all about.

As they approached a wooden bridge, their boat sliced across the canal, barely missing some gondolas and a highly polished *motoscafo* flying a crested flag. Then their boat slowed down, and the driver cut the motor.

"The *Accademia* Bridge. Our port of call."

The walk from the landing stage was dreamlike, a dream in which people under blue umbrellas at out-door cafés, people strolling, real cats, stone lions and

37

stone people on stone buildings (one, the sprawling Academy Museum) did not know they were watching a kidnapping. Indeed, she herself had all but forgotten about it.

They came to a quiet, narrow street of small stone houses with shuttered windows, awnings and balconies with flowerpots and birdcages. Under a tree, a cat ate spaghetti. Italy!

Agnes Grant banged on a wooden door with a huge brass knocker that was a lion's head. When the door was opened, a little dachshund came running.

"Siegfried . . . ?" Maggie inquired.

Siegfried was the one who had made Aunt Yvonne break her ankle when he ran off with the bath sponge. He was the reason Aunt Yvonne had not been in Genoa.

The little dog jumped up on her, and they kissed each other. Bingo! So she wasn't being kidnapped. (Now that that was settled, she felt a tiny nip of disappointment: *that* would have been some adventure!)

Maggie followed Agnes Grant into a whispering, creaking, dark interior, very foreign. The door had been opened by a dark woman in a dark dress. She nodded coldly at Maggie, and Maggie nodded nervously at her. (Traveling to foreign places where one did not speak foreign languages made for much nodding.) The woman disappeared.

Agnes Grant dropped Maggie's suitcase and yelled up the stairwell. "Okeydokey, no thanks to you, I found her."

She slapped Maggie on the back. "For such a skinny kid, you're real spunky. Have yourself a ball and don't get homesick like me."

"Thank you." Maggie suddenly loved Agnes Grant.

Agnes Grant turned and left.

"Maggie, Maggie . . . darling . . ."

The voice trilling down the stairwell was the actressy foggy one she had heard over the ship-to-shore phone. It was her Aunt Yvonne's.

Maggie picked up her suitcase; it did not weigh a feather; it was more like a sack of rocks.

The stairs were marble, but the carpet over them was threadbare. The paper on the wall showed signs of having once been silky red, now worn to shreds in spots. And the smell was old and it too hinted of a lovely past now gone musty.

Maggie bumped her bag up, step by step.

At the top of the stairs, Maggie stopped. There were so many doors.

"Here I am . . ."

Guided by the voice, Maggie entered a room where great gilt-framed mirrors, a crystal chandelier, and more gilt on the furniture also bespoke a lovely past, a past of tinkly music and minuets. It was a large room with a high ceiling, a kind of parlor and bed-room all in one.

A lady was stretched out on a chaise longue.

So this was Aunt Yvonne. The fairy godmother who had waved the wand that had turned her into a reluctant and scared-out-of-her-mind real adventuress. So this was Aunt Yvonne, whose real name was Mabel, and who had learned how not to be a provincial, and who had written many educational letters on the subject, filled with mixed metaphors, said her father.

Even with one black eye, she was pretty. And glitteringly blond. And flowing with chiffon. She looked awfully young to be a great-aunt, and she did not look as if she could possibly have come from Tilton, Iowa, which she did. That was before she went to Italy to become an opera star, which she did not. All she got to be was in the chorus.

"*Benvenuto—*" Aunt Yvonne sang in her throaty contralto and extended a fragile hand, heavily ringed.

Maggie went toward her, wide-eyed: This chif-fony, Italian-speaking lady was her *mother's* aunt? her woolly, cottony, windblown, silk-only-for-parties mother's aunt?

"You're here! You're here! Oh, thank the Lord! Really here, aren't you, darling?" (That sounded like a blood relative: hysterical.)

"I—I guess so."

40

"You poor darling," Aunt Yvonne said with a fluttery little laugh. "Come closer. I want to kiss you and to look at you."

Kissing Aunt Yvonne was like kissing a bouquet of flowers. But close up, there were tiny wrinkles around her eyes and mouth, which was sad because Aunt Yvonne didn't seem ready for them.

Maggie stood pigeon-toed for the inspection.

But Aunt Yvonne was dabbing at her eyes, the good one and the bad one.

"Oh, darling, don't mind me. You see you're *family* and home and . . . I've been gone such a long, long time . . . and I'm so happy to have you here . . ." Her voice trembled alarmingly.

Then, Aunt Yvonne breathed. That is to say, Aunt Yvonne performed the act of breathing. As she watched, Maggie's eyes got wider and wider. Aunt Yvonne closed her eyes and inhaled. She inhaled a lot. Then, she exhaled. A lot. She hissed as she did so. Then she inhaled again. Slowly. And a lot. Then her eyes flew open, and she smiled radiantly and waved her hand in the air. "Gone! The weepies! Gone! They can all keep their tranquilizers, I'll take breathing. Darling, I couldn't live without breathing. But that's because I'm a singer." The smile faded. "Was a singer." The smile lit up again. "I shall teach you breathing. Would you like that?"

Maggie nodded. Why not?

"Oh, darling, how lovely! You're open-minded! I was just a little worried that Tilton had made you . . . you know, somewhat narrow-minded and anti-breathing. If it hadn't been for breathing I never would have gotten through . . ." Aunt Yvonne winced.

Maggie glanced at the cast poking out of the chiffon and at the crutches close by and thought them marvelously romantic. Bandages were good, but casts and crutches were the best.

"Does it hurt a lot?" Maggie asked.

"What?"

"Your ankle. That one. You know, the one you broke?"

"Oh, that. To tell the truth, half the time I don't even know whether it hurts or not. That is, ever since—ever since the other unfortunate thing happened, the reason we're here in Venice instead of Cortina."

"Why are we here, Aunt Yvonne?"

"Oh, darling, it's too awful—"

Maggie expected Aunt Yvonne to breathe again, but she just shook her head and moaned softly.

"I'll tell you later, after you've unpacked. Oh, dear, I've been rattling on so. Darling, your poor little shoulder. Do put that bag down and let me look at you."

Maggie put the bag down, and Aunt Yvonne reached for her glasses on a table close by.

"Yes, yes, you've overcome it. More than that, I must confess you've made it charming . . . definitely charming . . ."

"Excuse me, Aunt Yvonne, but what is it I've overcome?"

"Your name, darling. The name, Maggie. I'm very

sensitive to names. When I was Mabel, I sang like a sick canary. As soon as I became Yvonne, I reached a perfectly beautiful C. Unfortunately, it wasn't soon enough for stardom, which is what worried me about you. Suppose, I wrote your mother—whom I adore, which is one of the reasons you're here—suppose the baby needs to feel like a Margherita to be what she wants to be? *Then* what?"

"What did my mother write back?"

"Oh, I've forgotten. I think it was something sassy like, 'then she should have picked an Italian mother.' Between you and me, I think she was quoting your father. A wonderful man—I adore him, too—but somewhat given to sarcasm."

(Which, Maggie remembered, is what her father thought Aunt Yvonne was given to.)

"I wish they'd listened to you. If I had a pretty name, it might help me know what I want to be. I change my mind every other minute."

"Do you now? That's interesting because I have an idea up my sleeve. We'll talk about it later. Now you'd better unpack and wash up. See that door there. That's your room. Close by."

Maggie went toward it.

"Darling—" Aunt Yvonne called after her.

"Yes?"

"It's very comforting having you here. Soothing, too."

44

"Thank you."

The room Maggie was to have to herself was a tiny one. It, too had a high ceiling, which was decorated with plaster flowers and vines, floor-length windows, faded flower wallpaper, a gigantic carved wardrobe (big enough to hold a family of ghosts), and a tiny daybed piled high with pillows and covered with a frayed silk counterpane. And a *dressing table* with a frilly skirt.

Maggie went to the window and pulled it open. To her delight, she saw that it overlooked a small garden, enclosed and tangled, where a live cat and a stone lion lay side by side as if they were in the Peaceable Kingdom, and where wisteria climbed a wall. From the porches of Tilton, Iowa, to a garden in Venice, Italy, was a long way for wisteria, like her, to have traveled. And beyond the garden was a strip of narrow, dark canal slipping past the flaking stone walls of ancient houses. This, then, was to be her own private view: she loved it.

Just before she turned back into the room, she heard the slapping of oars in the canal and a voice call out what sounded like "*Oi!*" There was another "*Oi!*" and a gondola appeared from around a corner.

Maggie turned back into the room and sighed deeply. It was a sigh of weariness, contentment, and anticipation; she loved this place: it was a place for laughing and singing and dancing; but beyond all else if she *was* going to have an adventure, this was the place to have it.

Aunt Yvonne had trouble telling what had happened. She cleared her throat a great deal and fiddled with her long string of pearls, which was wound around her neck before it dropped to her waist. Maggie was more involved in seeing whether Aunt Yvonne was going to break the string of pearls and send them flying all over the place than she was in her story. Her story was not all that new to Maggie. What it came down to was that Aunt Yvonne had become busted, but she couldn't come right out and say so the way her parents did. "Look, you kids," her mother would say to her and her brother, "we're absolutely busted this month, so would you *please* try not to spill, break, or lose anything until we can afford it again." Or something like that.

"And so I bought those dreadful debentures—" Aunt Yvonne was saying.

Debentures? Aunt Yvonne must mean *dentures,* and Maggie's eyes shot up from the pearls to Aunt Yvonne's teeth, which looked real.

But debentures, Maggie learned, were a very complicated and uninteresting way of losing money in real estate.

"And then when an unexpected and lovely offer came along to rent the house in Cortina, I remem-

46

bered that Signora Cavelli took in a paying guest or two and that you could have a lovely Venetian experience, so much more interesting, darling, than a Cortina experience. So dear, sturdy Agnes Grant, such an efficient woman, packed me up, drove me down and here I am. Here we are. Aren't we?" Aunt Yvonne sighed.

Thinking it was the moment to prove she was soothing, Maggie said soothingly, "Yes we are, Aunt Yvonne."

"Venice will be an education, darling. So much to see and do." Her face fell. "That won't cost money. Oh, dear . . ."

"Don't worry, Aunt Yvonne, I'm very good at being busted . . ."

That was reasonably true, but she had never before had to get home from Venice, Italy. If Aunt Yvonne couldn't afford the plane fare home, how would her parents be able to? They'd have to eat franks from now until Doomsday, and her mother would have to be really good *and* lucky at poker. Even so, at the stakes she and her friends played for, that might take until Doomsday too.

The question had to be asked: "Excuse me, please, Aunt Yvonne, but . . . but how am I going to get home?"

"How? Oh, you poor darling, you're worrying about the money for the ticket. That's all been taken care of, so don't give it another thought. Promise?"

"Uh-huh," Maggie muttered, not quite convinced that Aunt Yvonne was telling the truth.

Then Maggie remembered she was supposed to send another cable to her parents telling them she was safe again.

"They have a big thing about my being safe," she said.

"I must say, so have I," Aunt Yvonne retorted.

"But golly, it costs a pot to keep on repeating it. I had to send them a telegram from Kennedy Airport in New York, another from the ship before it sailed, and a cable when it arrived in Genoa. And now—"

"If you write the message down, Signora Cavelli will take care of sending it."

Maggie fetched a pencil and paper. She wet the pencil with the tip of her tongue, a sign that she was stuck.

"I don't know how to say I'm safe in Venice instead of Cortina in three words."

"Mm, that is rather a problem, isn't it? What about —'Safe in Venice, explanation follows'? That's five words. I don't think even Calvin Coolidge could have made it in three. Suppose I treat you to two."

"Oh, no thank you, I still have a little bit of money."

"Darling, the day I can't afford to give my one

48

and only great-niece two little words—"

"Okay. But the explanation better follow fast or my mother will have a fit. She has a terrific imagination for catastrophes."

Maggie found Signora Cavelli in the kitchen. In this kitchen, cabbages were not green or red but sapphire blue, and bean pods were dappled pink and white. A cook stood over a large copper pot of simmering water and scooped out little green balls as they floated to the surface. Sheets of sheer, silky dough were hanging over the backs of chairs, and at a large pastry board Signora Cavelli was slicing a sheet of dough into long, thin strips, using a knife at a dangerous speed.

Both women kept at their work while Maggie waited. The cook was the first to turn to Maggie. She smiled warmly: "*Gnocchi*," she said, pointing to the balls. (Maggie thought this word was spelled knee-ocky.)

Signora Cavelli did not smile. Girls were obviously not welcome in her kitchen. "Yes?" she asked.

Timidly, Maggie made her request. She also had the letter to Jasper to mail. (On the back of the envelope she had written "Surprise!" and the new address in Venice.)

Signora Cavelli impatiently consented to attend to the wire and the letter, then picked up another piece of dough.

As she left the kitchen, Maggie thought, "I'll never find out how to make spaghetti from *her*, but I hope I get to eat those *gnocchi*."

"Is Signora Cavelli always so grumpy?" Maggie asked Aunt Yvonne.

"Oh, don't mind her, darling. She's just not used to children. But I assured her that you were a perfectly lovely, quiet little girl and wouldn't be any trouble whatsoever. On the contrary, it was going to be a pleasure to have you—"

Since Aunt Yvonne had never seen her until this day, Maggie wondered how she had come to that conclusion. If her mother had made her out to be a goody-goody . . .

"And now here you are safe in Venice," Aunt Yvonne went on, looking more concerned than reassured, "Venice, such a ravishing place to be safe in, ravishing—"

It was hard to believe that this stagy lady was her own flesh and blood; being with her was going to be like being in a play that you made up as you went along. Some people in Tilton—like Diane who was a stickler for facts and figures—would call Aunt Yvonne a phony. Herself, she didn't mind phonies as long as they were nice. Aunt Yvonne was nice, and Maggie liked her.

They looked at each other; they smiled at each other; they looked away. Maggie knelt down and patted Siegfried, who turned over on his back with his paws waving in the air for more.

Maggie knew that in this awkward silence she and Aunt Yvonne were both wondering what Maggie was going to do all by herself in this ravishing place.

"Oh, darling, I did so want you with me. I had made such divine plans. In Cortina I had even found playmates for you. It was going to be a summer to remember all your life. And mine, too. An *Italian* summer. At your age to soak up beauty, art, the language, the food, the people—if only I had gotten Tilton out of me earlier—and *opera* . . . which reminds me, the little idea I had for your future?"

"Golly, I sure could use one."

"You *are* open-minded. I can't get over it. Tilton must have changed."

"Aunt Yvonne, Tilton may not be Venice, Italy, but it's okay."

"Bless your heart. Loyal, too. About my dream—I may as well call it by its true name—my dream for you . . . Darling—do you sing?"

"*Sing?*"

"Yes, you know—"

With which Aunt Yvonne sat up straight, took a deep breath, placed her hand on her diaphragm, and let loose with a most operatic trill up the scale. Siegfried cocked his head from side to side, and Maggie had a bad time stifling a giggle.

51

Aunt Yvonne frowned. "*That*, darling, was Mabel singing. She has a way of popping up in times of great stress. Oh, well—now let's hear Maggie. Now I do find it a charming name, and *that's* a compliment."

"Thanks a lot, but she can't sing worth a damn. She couldn't sing even if her name was Maria Callas."

"Ah, so you've heard of her have you?"

"Aunt Yvonne, Tilton isn't the jungle of New Guinea."

"I wish it had been. I could have taken that with more grace. As for Callas, the last time I heard her I'm sorry to say *she* sounded like Mabel. Come to think of it, do you suppose Maria is her real name?"

"I don't know. But changing names does seem to get people places. Barbra dropped an *a*."

"Barbara who, darling?"

"Barbara *who?* Golly, Aunt Yvonne! Barbra Streisand, of course. Now if I could sing like that . . ."

"Sing like a movie star? Darling, let's set our singing sights a bit higher than that, shall we?"

Maggie had an uneasy feeling that she had better cool Aunt Yvonne: *higher* than Barbra?

"Aunt Yvonne, I guess you'd better know about me. Sometimes all I want to be is a cheerleader or a girl detective." (She thought it best not to mention adventuress.)

"Cheerleader? Girl detective?" Aunt Yvonne trilled a little laugh. "I don't have anything against either of those as such. But if one is born with a gift, one must give it to the world, mustn't one? That's the least one can do, isn't it?"

"How do you know if the world wants it?"

"That I must say is a very good question. And to answer it truthfully, sometimes the world is plain ungrateful. But I don't want to talk about myself. Let me hear you sing."

"*Now?*"

"Not quite ready? Not in good voice?"

"No. I sure am not. I'd rather take Siegfried out for a walk instead. May I please?"

"Oh. Well, why not? Siegfried, darling, would you like to have a nice walk with Maggie?"

Siegfried, who had fallen asleep, opened one eye.

"Yes, he would," Aunt Yvonne said. Then, she worried: "Can you swim, darling?"

"Better than I can sing."

"That's a blessing. Then if you fall into a canal it will be all right. Only take my advice and don't, darling, they're frightfully smelly. Beautiful, but smelly. And there are no automobiles to worry about, so that's all right. And hardly any crime except for thievery. So from that point of view it's safe for you to get about. But—"

Maggie waited.

"But you have to get lost and then what?"

"Is getting lost a rule, Aunt Yvonne?"

"In Venice, everyone does. It's quite the thing to do. You see, Venice was settled by people who were hiding out and had no desire to be found. There are *rios*, which are canals, and *rioterras*, which used to be canals, and *campos*, which are small squares, and *campiellos*, which are smaller squares, and . . . and *vicolo ciecos*, which are blind alleys, so many blind alleys—such lovely names—I could go on and on—such a divine way to get lost—such an exquisite puzzle—" Aunt Yvonne stopped for breath, then went on in a nervous flutter: "But I can't have you getting lost. It would be too awful—"

"Everyone was always getting lost on the ship, too. But I used a map to find my way around it, and after ten days I was pretty good."

"You were? That *is* encouraging. I do have a map. Not that Venetian maps are reliable. The Venetians seem to get as confused as everyone else. But if you have this address with you—"

"And I can always ask, can't I?"

Aunt Yvonne looked pleased. "I knew it. I knew this trip would pay off for you. Maggie, you have become a born traveler."

Feeling like a fraud, Maggie accepted this compliment.

After Maggie and Aunt Yvonne studied a map, marked off the *Accademia* Bridge and what they were pretty sure was the general location of Signora

Cavelli's house, Aunt Yvonne had another worry:

"And darling, if you do have to get into conversation with someone—you know, about finding your way—I always trust Siegfried's judgment about people. If he doesn't like them, I don't. He always has a reason. If he growls at someone, go on your way, politely of course, but as fast as your legs can carry you. Not *everyone* in Venice is a Venetian, lovely and safe."

Siegfried did want to go for a walk until he had to have his muzzle put on. Then Maggie had to chase him all around the room.

"It's the one thing I do dislike about Venice, this law about muzzles. I suppose it's because they're so crazy about cats," Aunt Yvonne said indignantly.

When Siegfried was finally muzzled, Aunt Yvonne fluttered goodbye. "Don't be gone long, darling," she said with a nervous little laugh.

"I won't," Maggie assured her.

With Siegfried straining at the lead, Maggie stepped out into a Venetian early evening.

Before long, she discovered that everyone who wished to be lost in Venice was not.

4

It was like stepping into a pretend place, the most beautiful and mysterious that had ever been pretended. In the late afternoon sun, the shadows of stone animals, of a solitary tree, of the watery shadows of the little canal were all mysterious. But none more so than her own shadow on the narrow, cobbled lane. What was old Maggie's shadow doing there on a Venetian lane? And yet that shadow that glided and wiggled and stood still was more real than old Maggie was.

As she walked, Maggie heard the *clop-clop* of heels on the stone flagstones, other people's, and the echo of her own. She heard birds chirping, cups and glasses tinkling at the outdoor cafés, voices behind shuttered windows, laughter from gondolas, the roar of a motorboat, a ship's siren in the distance, Venetian sounds.

As she walked, Maggie tried to leave a trail of land-marks behind her—a church, a wellhead, a little café, a particularly crazy-looking lion, a *campiello*, a bridge, and a *vicolo cieco*.

As he walked, moving like a mechanical toy on his short little legs, Siegfried kept his muzzled nose raised haughtily. When he saw a cat, he paused only long enough to lift one paw and give it a baleful eye before moving on. The cats of Venice for their part seemed too well entrenched to worry about dogs, par-ticularly muzzled ones.

Maggie had come to another little canal and was watching two gondolas with fringed canopies about to collide when she thought she heard her name called. The gondoliers were shouting at each other and over the shouts she thought she heard "Mag-gie . . . Mag-gie." Which was crazy.

But the call persisted and she looked around fran-tically. It was a boy's voice, and she had the wild hope that it might be Jasper, miraculously grounded in Venice.

Then she spotted a boy and a girl. With an unrea-sonable stab of disappointment, she saw it wasn't

Jasper. It was Pietro, an Italian boy who had been on the *Toscana* with her. He was one of a group Maggie and Jasper had gone around with. She had forgotten that Pietro was Venetian and that she knew

someone in Venice. He was jumping up and down excitedly. She too jumped up and down yelling "Pietro," which made Siegfried bark as hysterically as he could behind his muzzle.

Pietro, who only knew a few words of English, shouted to Maggie in Italian.

"What?" Maggie shouted back.

The girl cupped her mouth: "Stay there. Stay where you are. We'll come to you."

Pietro and the girl disappeared into an alley, one of the thousands of alleys of Venice. Maggie had already learned that in Venice it was going to be useful to be skinny: she had just seen two fat women unable to pass each other in an alley.

When streets are made of water, to get to someone just a few yards away from you takes some doing if there is no bridge at hand. It also takes an expert at winding in and out of lanes and alleys to get there fast.

Presently, Maggie heard the loud *clop-clopping* of racing feet. Siegfried yelped as Pietro and the girl skidded to a stop. In the manner of people who have just made a journey together, Maggie and Pietro were overjoyed to see each other. Their way of expressing this was by laughing uproariously, as if the laughter itself would recall all the fun they had had together on the ship.

The girl eyed Maggie up and down, stroked Siegfried, and waited for them to stop.

Pietro poked his finger at the girl. "She, Emilia. She, cousin."

"He sounds like Tarzan, is it not so? Me, Tarzan . . ." Emilia punched her chest. "Actually, Pietro knows more English than he thinks, but I shall be his interpreter."

"You speak English well," Maggie said, relieved.

"I jolly well ought to. I have just been to school in England."

"I can tell you didn't learn it in Iowa."

Pietro leaned over to pet Siegfried. Siegfried bared his teeth and growled.

"Goodness!" Maggie said, yanking him back.

Pietro tried again. This time Siegfried growled and tried to snap.

"Goodness gracious!" Maggie exclaimed and began to laugh. "Siegfried, stop that! Pietro *is* Venetian and he's not the least bit criminal. Are you, Pietro?"

Pietro looked bewildered. Maggie turned to Emilia. She, too, looked bewildered.

"It's a joke," Maggie said, and explained that Aunt Yvonne had warned her to beware of people Siegfried didn't like.

Emilia listened seriously and examined Pietro's ear lobes. Then she shook her head. "He has none. Pietro is perhaps a latent criminal."

"Me is what?" Pietro asked.

61

"You are *criminale*."

This delighted Pietro whose hands became guns as he went, "Bang! Bang! Bang!"

This enraged Siegfried who had to be calmed down, and earned Pietro a dressing down from Emilia.

"Pietro is immature," Emilia said.

Pietro grinned.

"No Cortina?" he asked Maggie.

"No Cortina. Aunt Yvonne got—" Maggie turned to Emilia. "How do you say busted in Italian?"

"Busted? What is it busted?" Emilia asked.

"Busted is when you are not exactly poor but don't have any money most of the time."

Emilia and Pietro were properly sympathetic, rather perplexed, but also frankly happy to be meeting their first busted friend. Unfortunately, everyone they knew had a certain amount of money always, which was not as interesting as being busted. But wasn't it unusual for an American to be busted? Weren't all Americans rich? Maggie assured them that this was not so.

"Pietro says to tell you it will be our pleasure to have the honor to steal food from our house for you if it is necessary," Emilia said with some formality, and added with a little smile, "The little dog perhaps has second sight."

"Oh, that's very nice of you, but I don't think we're starving busted. At least I hope we're not. I think we're just ordinary busted."

This disappointed Pietro.

"Pietro likes very much excitement. He wishes to race cars when he grows up."

"But there are no cars in Venice."

"Exactly."

"Oh."

"On the way here Pietro told me about you. He said you were rather famous on the ship coming over."

Maggie shrugged. "Oh, well . . ."

"He said you were very frightened at the first."

Maggie frowned. "Mm—I guess you could call it that." There was no point in denying it, but to have the *whole world* talking about it . . .

"But that you also liked adventure. Is that true?"

Maggie brightened. "Yes, it is. I guess I'm hooked on it."

Emilia inspected Maggie carefully. "To look at you one would not suspect you of this addiction."

Maggie did not take that as a compliment, but she decided to laugh it off. She raised one eyebrow (a recent accomplishment) and said in a deep, pretend foreign voice, "It is because, *signorina*, I am traveling incognito in drip-dries." In her own voice, she added, "In drip-dries? Ugh!"

Emilia laughed and translated all this to Pietro and he did a cartwheel, which almost sent him into a canal.

"You see how he likes the excitement. Pietro is an

extrovert. Myself I am an introvert. I am very interested in psychology. Also in needlepoint. So—" Emilia became businesslike, "we three are now friends. I have never had before an American friend. Where are you staying?"

Maggie dug into her bag and brought out the address.

"Aunt Yvonne says we're paying guests. At home, we would be boarders."

"Signora Cavelli she is also probably busted. It pleases me very much the word busted. We three will have a jolly time of it."

Pietro and Emilia lived only several bridges, *calles*, *cortes* (which Aunt Yvonne had not mentioned), and, of course, alleys away from Maggie, and before too long she would find her way there without too much trouble. They lived in separate flats in the family house. They would show Maggie all of Venice, and they would also take her out in a gondola, and go to the Lido, where they would swim, and around the lagoons and most wonderful of all to the cemetery . . .

"Cemetery . . . ?" Maggie's voice quavered.

"Don't you like cemeteries?"

"Mm."

"You are afraid of the dead?" There was genuine disbelief on Emilia's face.

"Mm—I do sort of like live people better."

Pietro and Emilia became rather grand.

"But in Venice we have the most beautiful funerals in the world—the *motoscafos*—the gilded barge—the weeping lion—it is all gloriously beautiful—and the cemetery island of San Michele it is sadly beautiful and our family tomb it is tragically beautiful. Pietro and I, we are fond of sitting in the family tomb and telling terrible stories about death—murders. We find it jolly and beautiful—" Emilia smiled encouragingly, "and so will you."

Maggie had to remind herself that she was seeking adventure.

"Oh, I'm quite sure I will," she said, airily, "but I think I'd better go back now, or my aunt will think I'm lost. Which I hope I'm not. Golly, now I can't remember whether I came from the left or right . . ."

"Would you like us to lead you back?"

"Oh, thank you, that would be great!"

"We shall go a good way."

The good way turned into a maze of alleys, lanes, and bridges that thoroughly confused Maggie and also made her dizzy. The only familiar landmark was the crazy lion.

When they reached Signora Cavelli's house, Maggie thought it only polite to invite Emilia and Pietro in.

"But—" she warned, "the *signora* is not used to kids."

Emilia and Pietro nodded knowingly.

This time, fortunately, it was the cook who opened the door. She beamed.

Emilia and Pietro, for their part, were not used to an Aunt Yvonne with a black eye and a leg in a cast. They were frankly fascinated and unable to stop gawking.

And Maggie was proud of possessing such an aunt. As she lay on the chaise in the spotlight of the setting sun, Aunt Yvonne was definitely worth showing off. More so, when she and Emilia began to rattle away in Italian.

"Maggie, darling," Aunt Yvonne said, "what good luck for you to have run into such delightful companions!" With a larger audience, Aunt Yvonne was getting stagier and stagier. "But then in Venice, it really isn't luck. It's inevitable. It's because in Venice one is always walking. Emilia says she will be delighted to show you around. With you in such good hands, I will now completely relax."

Pietro whispered to Emilia. Emilia shook her head.

"What is it that he wants, dear?" Aunt Yvonne asked.

"He would like very much to try your crutches."

"But of course," Aunt Yvonne responded expansively. "Be my guest."

Siegfried, however, objected. Pietro took off around the room on the crutches like a speed maniac, as if he had been on crutches all his life. Siegfried pointed his nose toward the ceiling and wailed like a banshee.

"No! No! Siegfried!" Aunt Yvonne was laughing and scolding at the same time. "Signora Cavelli will throw us out."

Indeed, at the sound of heavy footsteps, Pietro dropped the crutches in haste and Siegfried stopped wailing.

When Emilia and Pietro left, Maggie went with them. Emilia would show Maggie around the neighborhood and the way to the *Accademia* Bridge, which was to be their meeting place in the future.

"And soon," Aunt Yvonne had coaxed, "you children will stop in to see the Giorgiones and the Carpaccios and the Titians at the *Accademia*, won't you?"

"*Si, si*," Emilia had responded lukewarmly.

Outside, she said: "Your aunt she is very amusing. I like her in spite of her compulsion to stuff you with art. In Venice, there is much for us to do before museums. We must go certainly to the Piazza."

"What is the piazza?"

"What is the *Piazza?*" Emilia was amazed. "There is only one piazza in the world. That is the Piazza of *San Marco*—Saint Mark. Wait until you see it! Then you will see something."

But presently, Maggie saw something of more

immediate interest to her.

They were passing through a narrow lane with two small markets, one displaying a rainbow of vegetables, the other dried beans, cheeses, bread, and the like.

It was not the food that made Maggie catch her breath. It was the hippie mother, Vicky. She came out of the grocery store carrying a well-filled shopping bag.

"Hi—" Maggie said, her eyes on the bread and milk sticking out of the bag.

It was a very narrow lane and they were, at the most, two feet away from each other.

But Vicky rushed past Maggie as if she had never seen her before in her life and disappeared around a corner.

"Wow!"

"Wow what? Have you never seen a hippie before?" Emilia asked.

"That's just it. I bumped knees with this one all the way from Genoa to Venice. What is she doing in Venice when she said she was going to Trieste?"

"Perhaps she, too, became busted."

"N-no. I somehow don't think so. And why did she pretend she didn't know me? Why?"

"Perhaps she is on a trip?"

"Trip?"

"You know—under the influence of a dangerous drug—"

Maggie shook her head. "No. I have an awful feeling—Come on! Why are we standing here? Let's follow her. Quick!"

They, too, rounded the corner into another lane, but there was no sight of Vicky.

Maggie studied the two rows of houses lining the lane: where shuttered windows was the prevailing custom, houses became good hiding places.

And Emilia studied Maggie with professional interest. "See here, you aren't by any chance pretending to be a girl detective or some such thing?"

The question being uncomfortably near right, Maggie didn't answer it.

"I sure wish Jasper were here," she said.

"Is he your boyfriend?" Emilia asked.

"He is a boy, and he is a friend, a very good friend. And he is also the smartest boy I know, and that is why I wish he were here because he would know what to do."

"You're blushing you know."

"I am not. I'm just excited." Maggie hated people to say she was blushing when she was. It only made her blush more.

Pietro was talking and tugging at Emilia's sleeve.

"*Non so*," Emilia brushed him off irritably. "He wants to know what this is all about, and I told him I don't know. Are you going to tell? I am not myself too stupid."

"I can see that." But Maggie still took her time. "It's that I'm suspicious of—"

"Of *what?*"

Maggie hesitated. It was now more than a suspicion. Maggie dropped her voice. "Of a kidnapping."

"A *keednapping!*" Emilia and Pietro exclaimed together.

"Shh! Don't shout about it."

"And who is the person who is supposed to be kidnapped?" Emilia asked, highly skeptical.

"Charlie."

"*Charlie?* Aren't you being rather familiar? I thought myself I was in love with Charles, but I recovered."

"Who is Charles?"

"Who is Charles? Charles is only the present Prince of Wales of England. Who is Charlie?"

"Charlie is a baby."

"Oh."

They giggled over the case of mistaken identity.

"Charlie was on the train with them, and it's all very peculiar."

"It is not that I wish to be rude, but is it not the possibility that you Americans have the phobia about crime because you have it so much? So always you have it on the mind?"

"In Tilton, Iowa, we don't have crime," Maggie flared patriotically. "Not much that is."

"You have not been mugged?"

Maggie burst out laughing. "Golly! In Tilton? Of course not. I think muggers have to be strangers, and we don't have any. Honestly, your opinion of us Americans—"

It was Emilia's turn to flare patriotically. "But you see we Italians we do not even have our own word for kidnapping. We use yours. That is why Pietro knew it. We do not have a word because it is not the Italian custom to kidnap. But do not let us fight about these national differences. Let us discuss the case. What are the clues? What is it that was so peculiar?"

Maggie listed the clues and ended with ". . . and that baby didn't act as if these hippies were his real parents."

"That is not enough to go to the police with. It is possible they are not his parents. But it is also possible they are good friends doing a favor to the parents."

"Per-haps—but if that's so, Charlie's parents have very peculiar good friends. Mighty peculiar."

"That is not a crime. That is just a poor selection of friends," Emilia said.

By this time, they had reached the *Accademia* Bridge.

"So then, we three friends who are not peculiar should meet tomorrow, here in the afternoon?" Emilia suggested.

"What is it pee-culiar?" Pietro wished to know.

Emilia explained in Italian.

Pietro thumped himself on the chest. "Me, Pietro, me like peculiar."

"Me, Maggie, me do, too," Maggie admitted under her breath, because wasn't it the stuff that adventures were made of?

"*Ciao*," Emilia and Pietro called to Maggie as they parted. "*Ciao*," she called back. They were friends now, and Maggie thought that with these foreign friends she must be well on her way to being a cosmopolitan person.

But as she walked away alone, Maggie looked up at the darkening Venetian sky and murmured, "*Ciao*, Jasper." Jasper would understand why she was worried about Charlie. He was that kind of boy.

The dinner hour at Signora Cavelli's, delightfully foreign and late, presented Aunt Yvonne and Maggie with a problem. At lunch, before Maggie had arrived, Aunt Yvonne had stood at the top of the stairs on her crutches and decided that death by starvation was to be preferred to death from a broken neck. Getting up the stairs had been bad enough, but she could not, would not go down them to eat in the dining room. Agnes Grant had carried a tray from the kitchen.

"I do so hate to ask Signora Cavelli—" Aunt Yvonne said.

"That makes two of us," Maggie answered quickly.

"I'll carry a tray, Aunt Yvonne. I'll carry lots of trays. Breakfast, lunch, and dinner. Up and down with everything."

Aunt Yvonne's good eye opened wide. "How very dear of you, how very, very dear—"

Maggie lowered her eyes modestly. "Trays for both of us, Aunt Yvonne."

"Oh, darling, I do think Signora Cavelli would expect you to eat with her."

Maggie's eyes flew upward wildly. "Aunt Yvonne! *I'll* die of starvation if I have to eat alone with Signora Cavelli. My throat will close up. My stomach will close up. And I most likely will throw up."

"But why, darling?"

Maggie shrugged. "The lady spooks me." Maggie thought her smile was called for. "*Please?*"

"But up and down the stairs with all those trays— and so slender—you'll fade away. And I did promise your mother I would take good care of you—"

"My mother loves it when I carry trays. She thinks it's adorable. Honestly."

"Well, it is dear of you, and we'll see what Signora Cavelli has to say."

To no one's surprise, Signora Cavelli approved of a child making herself useful, but worried about her china, her rugs, and her furniture. Also her floors and walls. Also the food, every beautiful morsel of which was precious. Nothing was to be spilled!

Nothing! Climbing the stairs with the first tray laden with *Zuppa di Peoci* (Venetian mussel soup) and *gnocchi* and salad, Maggie's tongue definitely poked out and her eyes glazed as they watched some mussels float back and forth to the very edge of a soup bowl. Mt. Everest, she thought, had nothing over these stairs.

But the next hour was filled with miracles: Maggie made all the trips without spilling a drop; she ate her first mussel and, to her amazement, survived the slithery experience to eat the rest with gusto; and lastly, there was the miracle of plain, old humdrum spinach turning into delectable dumplings called *gnocchi.*

After Maggie returned the last tray to the kitchen, told the cook in sign language how delicious everything had been, and received the grudging admission by Signora Cavelli that *this* time there had been no accidents, she said a sleepy goodnight to Aunt Yvonne.

Aunt Yvonne sighed with contentment. "I hope you are as happy to be here as I am to have you, darling. The children, Emilia and Pietro, do seem attractive and I see you having lovely, peaceful Venetian days together. Don't you?"

"Mm . . . sort of . . ."

"When you come down to it, peace and quiet is what I am beginning to cherish most—" Aunt Yvonne yawned and her eyelids drooped.

And Maggie thought that if peace and quiet were what Aunt Yvonne cherished, there was no point in waking her up to tell about her own opposite preference for high adventure, or to tell about Charlie and hippies and *kidnapping*.

Before getting into bed, Maggie opened her window and peered down into the garden and beyond it to the canal. The garden was strongly scented, the canal was dappled with moonbeams, the dark shadow of a gondola drifted by. Seen through eyes half-asleep, the Venetian night was gauzelike.

Maggie sank into the soft bed. After eleven nights of being rocked to sleep on the ship, the stillness of this bed was strange. So was her last waking thought: Where was little old Charlie sleeping?

5

THE NEXT MORNING, WHILE WALKING SIEGFRIED,
Maggie discovered that indeed Venice was a place for
meeting old acquaintances.

In a way, it was not too surprising to meet this
acquaintance. It was his business to move rapidly
from city to city, sometimes from country to country. The day before yesterday, it had been Naples.
Today, Venice. Tomorrow . . . who knew? It was
Signor T, the man from Interpol, who had been a
friend when she and Jasper needed one, when they
were both "unaccompanied minors" and in trouble.

At sight of him, Maggie's first thought was that she was seeing things. But there he was, fat as ever (there was no reason for him to have become skinny in a couple of days), sitting at an outside table of a *trattoria* reading a newspaper.

Maggie ran toward him, and it was Siegfried's barking at finding himself suddenly running that made Signor T look up.

For one awful second Maggie thought that he, too, was going to pretend not to know her: his face was blank.

"Hi—" Maggie called out.

"Ah—hi—" Signor T expressed neither enthusiasm nor surprise at seeing Maggie. He too took it for granted that Venice was the meeting place of the world. But Maggie was taken aback; when they had parted in Naples, he had been warm and friendly.

"And why are you not in Cortina?" Signor T asked professionally. It was his business to know whether people were where they were supposed to be.

When Maggie told him, he became sympathetic.

"So—it is a big inconvenience to lose much money." Signor T spoke just above a whisper; barely moving his lips, he still made himself understood. "I will be obliged if you do not tell of my identity to anyone. Your auntie, too. Yes?"

Now Maggie understood his coolness, and her

heart began to pound.

"I get it. You are here—on business?"

"Precisely."

Maggie moved her chair closer.

"I may have some business for you, too." Maggie discovered that she, too, could talk without moving her lips, although it gave her a growly feeling in her chest.

Behind his glasses, Signor T's eyes glinted.

"Tsk-tsk. You have become addicted to adventure?"

"Sort of."

Signor T sighed. "I know well how it is. But remember, Signorina Maggie, that always it does not end up with the pizzas and the water ices." (This was a reference to the treats he had given Maggie and Jasper in Naples.) "Which reminds me, you would like perhaps to join me with an *espresso?*"

Maggie was pleased with herself; from her trip over on an Italian ship she knew that *espresso* was not a train or some scary food like an eel or a baby octopus or some poor little lark Aunt Yvonne had told her Venetians were fond of eating, but a coffee. She also was pleased that Signor T considered her grown up enough for an *espresso*.

So it was over an *espresso* (which Maggie thought tasted like poison and had trouble swallowing) that she told Signor T of her suspicions about Charlie.

Involved though she was in the telling, Maggie longed for a camera to register this moment for posterity. If only all of Tilton, but particularly her best friend Diane, could see her now, sitting at an outdoor café, drinking an *espresso* (she took a sip) with a man from Interpol, *discussing business*. With a dachshund at her feet.

The man from Interpol listened just the way they did in mysteries—impassively. It was lovely the way real life was acting like a whodunit.

"You have read perhaps a book too many," Signor T said, reading her mind in a creepy way. "You understand it is not so much clues that you describe, but behavior. This is not to say that a surreptitious nudge is not sometimes more significant than is a bloody knife. A nudge can signify a serious crime. A bloody knife it can signify merely that the beef was too tough, the knife was too sharp, and the carver was inexperienced. It is the method of Simenon's Maigret, you know, to consider human behavior before the circumstantial clue. It is a method I myself prefer."

Maggie was leaning so far forward toward this priceless lesson she almost fell off the chair.

"Ooh—"

"Now, *signorina*, where was this *drogheria*, this grocery?"

"Um—let me think—there was this crazy lion—"

"Venice has a large population of crazy lions."

"Oh, golly—well, it wasn't far from where I live. I guess I should have written it down?"

"*Signorina*, one does not learn this business overnight. But, never mind, there is no reason to believe that these hippies they are still here in Venice."

That was not at all reassuring. The idea of their having vanished with Charlie was truly disquieting to Maggie.

Quick to note this, Signor T said, "On the other hand, they may still be here, and it is best that you know where to reach me."

"Oh, thank you, Signor T."

"T? Very good."

He tore a page from a notebook and scribbled on it. "It is my *pensione*. They will know who T is. Where is it that you stay?"

Maggie began to dig in her bag. Signor T waited patiently until a crumpled piece of paper finally turned up. After he had copied Maggie's address in his notebook, he said: "It is recommended that you keep this more at hand. It goes without saying in Venice you will get lost. To get home, you will show this paper to Venetians. Each one will direct you in another way. It does not matter if they do not know the way. Venetians they always know best. Eventually, in spite of the help, you will arrive at home. And whichever way you get there, it will be for the eyes a joy." Signor T sighed. "Ah, to be young and lost in Venice. I envy you, *signorina*."

"Don't *you* get lost?"

Signor T shook his head. "It is one of the sadnesses of my profession that we are not permitted the pleasure of being lost—anywhere."

He looked at his watch and pursed his lips. "Now I must to go." Signor T, who was very fat, lifted himself out of the chair with a remarkable display of grace and control, as if he were as light as a feather. He left some lire on the table and said, once again without moving his lips, "Please to not follow me—"

In a rush of excitement, Maggie whispered back, "If I can help *you* again, now you know where to get me—"

"It is kind of you. But again I warn you to take care with your addiction to adventure . . ."

Maggie found a postcard in her bag and then and there wrote to Jasper:

P.S.!!! Guess who I just ran into?!!! I'll give you a hint. Meeting him was spooky because of what I just wrote you!!! And I may need his help! Fantastic may not be the right word for Venice but it sure fills me full of!!!!!!!!

In the early afternoon, Maggie met Emilia and Pietro at the *Accademia* Bridge, and Maggie had a hard time keeping quiet about Signor T. Even a Venetian would have to be impressed; it wasn't everyone who personally knew a man from Interpol.

"So—what is it you would like best to do?" Emilia asked.

"Could we please first go back around where that grocery store is?"

"You have still the kidnapping on the mind?"

"Of course I do," Maggie retorted. "Kidnapping isn't something you forget like—like your umbrella or your gloves."

"What makes you think that already she would be back at that store?"

"I don't know." Maggie paused. "Maybe she forgot something. My mother always does."

"Maybe if you are right and she is a kidnapper, exactly because she *did* see you, she will not go back there. Eh?"

It annoyed Maggie that she had not been the one to think of that.

"Maybe yes and maybe no. I still would like to go."

"Very well. And if you see her, what will you do?"

Maggie hesitated. "Mm. Oh, I'll think of something—"

Emilia regarded Maggie with interest. "You are a born optimist?"

"*Born?* Oh, no. I'm a self-made optimist who's very easily changed back into a pessimist. And you?"

"I have not yet decided. But what if by following her you make this kidnapper suspicious that she has been found out, and then she wishes to get rid of you?"

Maggie stopped walking.

"*Rid?*"

"Rid." Emilia ran her finger across her throat.

"Golly! You have too decided. That's the most pessimistic idea I ever heard anyone have about me."

"I am often a realist. Do you wish to change your mind?"

Maggie thought of Vicky's dark, dark glasses. They were sort of sinister, weren't they? Then she thought she was very young to be gotten rid of, before she had even had a chance to get older.

"Well?" Emilia prodded.

"I'm still thinking . . ."

Then she thought of Charlie, cute little Charlie—whom she wished she hadn't thought of. But it was remembering Signor T that clinched it.

"Come on. Just because she's a kidnapper, doesn't mean she's a murderer."

"You are either brave or stupid."

"Thanks. Thanks a lot."

"I apologize. Instead of stupid, more polite would be immature."

"Double thanks."

Maggie followed Emilia and Pietro as they led the way back to the grocery store. They wandered in and out of alleys and up and down little bridges, and it crossed Maggie's mind that they were showing off by making the way needlessly complicated. Once, Pietro got involved with some boys in a running game in the courtyard of a magnificent palace until Emilia made him stop. "Do these boys *live* here?" Maggie asked, awed, and wondering whether the boys were princes incognito. Emilia laughed.

"These boys? No, it's just a favorite running place. Boys have to run someplace."

Growing up in Venice, Maggie thought, must be altogether different from growing up in Tilton.

When they reached the entrance to the lane where the *drogheria* was, they slowed down, and—either by design or accident—Emilia and Pietro fell behind Maggie, making her the leader. Maggie settled her bag on her shoulder, flipped back her hair, and became nonchalant. Becoming nonchalant worked from the outside in: if you looked it, you became it. Sometimes. As far as she personally was concerned, if this educational trip taught her how to be nonchalant, Aunt Yvonne's money wouldn't be wasted.

Suddenly, Pietro made a hissing noise, and Maggie lost her nonchalance with a gasp. Emilia gasped, too.

"*What?*" they both asked in stage whispers.

"There!" Pietro pointed down the lane.

Emilia and Maggie looked, goggle-eyed. There was nothing to see.

Pietro grinned. "Ha! Ha! Ha!"

Maggie longed to hit him on the head with her bag. Emilia scolded him and said to Maggie: "Pietro, he is exceedingly immature."

Pietro thumped himself on his chest. "Me, Pietro. Me, immature. Ha! Ha! Ha!"

"He, Pietro, he on big ego trip?" Maggie asked Emilia.

"Precisely," Emilia said, smiling.

Then they became serious and sleuthed down the

lane. To do so, they pretended to be playing a no stepping-on-the-crack game (which was difficult on such small squares of pavement), as they shot searching glances down side alleys and into doorways and even into an unshuttered ground-floor window.

"*Avanti! Avanti!*" A housewife, overloaded with string shopping bags, urged them to get out of her way.

"*Scusi, scusi,*" they all chorused (which made Maggie feel quite Venetian).

There was no sign of Vicky, Mike, or Charlie.

"Perhaps we should ask in the grocery store if they've seen Vicky again?" Maggie suggested.

Emilia thought about this. "I would have to be the one to ask?"

Maggie nodded. "You or Pietro."

Emilia thought some more. "The man being Venetian he would want to know why do I wish to know about a hippie? I would not have an answer. I would turn to you. You would also not have an answer—"

"Oh, yes I would. I would say I traveled with her on the train and I dropped something out of my bag —which, believe me, could be the honest truth—and I want to know if she saw it . . . by some chance . . ."

"By no chance would he believe it. Being Venetian he would be suspicious."

"Emilia! Being Venetian, you just don't want to

86

do it, isn't that so?"

"It is so. But it is not that I am Venetian. It is that you wish to be a detective. Myself, I consider to be a psychologist. A detective, he snoops outside the person, a psychologist, he snoops inside."

"Maigret snoops outside and inside. But okay, if poor little Charlie . . ."

Emilia sighed. "Come on."

As they crossed the threshold of the store, Maggie began to lose her nerve. She also had a disturbing second thought: Suppose Vicky walked in and found them there? Wouldn't she get suspicious?

"No," Maggie said, very loud. "I changed my mind. I don't want any—" she looked around wildly —"any beans."

They turned and stumbled out.

Outside, Maggie set them off into a great fit of giggles. When they stopped, she explained her change of mind.

Emilia approved: "So clever. You will make perhaps a famous detective."

As they retraced their steps out of the lane, Maggie, planning to return by herself, took careful note of the surroundings.

"Now—" Emilia asked, "are you truly burning to see art?"

"Mm. Not exactly. What else do you have in mind?"

"I have in mind San Michele, the cemetery. We can pick up the *vaporetto* and we can stay there for an hour or so. You will find it beautiful and terrifying, yes? Will she not, Pietro?"

Pietro sucked his cheeks in and made himself as cadaverous looking as possible. Then he grinned: "Maggie, she love adventure, she love San Michele."

"And do we *sit* in the family tomb?" Maggie asked in a small voice.

"But of course, that's the best part," Emilia answered. "That's where you get the most marvelous goose pimples."

"Oh."

Once again, Maggie went into her nonchalant routine and, with a majestic wave of her hand, said, "*Avanti!*"

They went back to the bridge where there was a *vaporetti* station. Taking the proper amount of lire from Maggie, Emilia took charge of getting them on a *vaporetto*. Emilia reported that when she told the conductor they were going to San Michele, he had approved mournfully. "It is respectful to visit the dead," he had said, and she had mournfully agreed.

The *vaporetti* are squat, roofed-over boats that chug up and down the canals of Venice and are water-buses for the Venetians.

This one was jammed, but Pietro wriggled through the crowd to get to the little glass-enclosed wheelhouse, and Maggie and Emilia squeezed in next to the rail, where Maggie had a fine view of the Grand Canal. When they stopped at the Piazzetta San Marco, Maggie had a glimpse of the great Basilica of St. Mark and a close-up of the Doge's Palace.

"Wow!" Maggie exclaimed. "All this for a duke who was not even a king?"

"But of course. Those doges were highly kingly. But myself, I prefer my house less grand and more safe. Here were doges murdered, executed, blinded, exiled. *Our* past, it was bloody as could be, and quite filled with the most up-to-date horrible tortures," Emilia bragged.

Not to be outdone, Maggie said: "Don't forget we had a revolution and a civil war ourselves and hanging of witches and scalping of people . . ."

"Poo! I do not wish to be snobbish, but you must agree that your tortures were not as grand as ours. Here on the Piazzetta and on the upper columns of the palace, citizens were hanged and we had much quartering, beheading, and strangling—"

"Okay, okay. Your past may have been more *gorgeously* gory, but ours was no picnic—" Maggie grinned—"although it did have a tea party."

"Tea party?"

"That's a joke. A historical joke."

The competition stopped when the *vaporetto* took off again.

But when they approached the island of San Michele, Emilia said, in a funereal voice, "This is the *laguna morta*, the lagoon of the dead, and you know, there are places in the lagoon where are the bones of the corpses of our past—"

Pietro returned just in time to crack his knuckles in Maggie's ear, which made her shriek, much to Pietro's satisfaction.

The island, drifting toward them as if it was sad and lonely, was walled and funereal with cypress trees, and beautiful.

When Maggie set foot on the island, she felt herself begin to go clammy. True, there were beautiful flowers among the tombs, monuments, and cypress trees, but *so many* dead people and *pictures* of some!

And when they reached the marble mausoleum that belonged to Emilia and Pietro's family, Maggie thought she herself would die if she had to enter its cold, cold marble interior.

Maggie had not called upon herself as She, the Adventuress, in some days, not since she had gotten so attached to real live adventure. She did so now: She, the Adventuress, being, to the best of her knowledge, perfectly alive is about to cross the River Styx to the world of the dead. And sure wishes she weren't.

Emilia nudged her.

"Does—does anyone live here?" Maggie whispered. "I mean is anyone—you know—inside?"

"Yes," Emilia whispered back.

"Oh, golly! Who?"

"Our great-grandfather and our great-grand-mother."

"Don't they—won't they—I mean—how do you know they don't mind our butting in?"

"They don't. They're Venetians. They're used to being dead."

Emilia gave Maggie a shove.

Inside it was icy cold. There were two wrought iron benches and a table, and doors in the walls, which Maggie hastily turned away from, and portraits of a man and a woman. Maggie took one quick look at them and decided they did so mind the intrusion. Silently, swiftly, she apologized to them and dropped her eyes.

"So—" Emilia said, in a sepulchral whisper, "is not it beautiful here?"

Maggie's neck being stiff, she nodded with some effort.

"Pr-r-etty. But not what I'd call cozy."

"But mournful. Beautiful and mournful. So, please, *si accomidi*—make yourself at home." Emilia pointed to a bench.

"Not yet. I hope," Maggie whispered, sitting down gingerly on the edge of the bench.

Pietro was making cadaverous faces and squirming. "Begin the terrible tales," he urged in an extremely sepulchral whisper.

"*Si, si . . .*" Emilia appeared to be working herself into a trance from which the terrifying tales would come forth.

Watching her, Maggie was aware that the goose pimples Emilia had promised were already sprouting from the cold damp surface of her skin, sprouting before she had heard one terrifying word. And then quite unexpectedly she remembered that the best defense was an offense.

"Ooh—" Maggie moaned, and then covered her mouth.

"What is it?" Emilia asked, sharply.

"Did you hear something?"

"*What?*"

"Sh-h-h!"

Pietro had stopped making faces and moved closer to Emilia.

"Don't you hear—a knocking, knocking, knocking?"

"No, I don't hear. Pietro, do you hear?"

Pietro did not answer.

"I hear it," Maggie whispered. "Once there was a lady—" She shuddered. It was a genuine shudder.

"What lady?" Emilia asked, in a frightened whisper.

"Her name was Madeline. And—and she was buried—" Maggie stopped.

"So?" Emilia stiffened.

"Alive. Buried alive." Maggie could barely say it.

Emilia and Pietro caught their breath.

"And then, one terrible dark and stormy night, there was this knocking-knocking and then terrible noises —scraping-scraping—and then—" Maggie stopped again. "And then, it was too terrible. Should I stop?"

Emilia and Pietro didn't answer.

It was Pietro who said: "I hear. I hear. The knocking."

"I—I—me, too—" Emilia croaked.

"And then—" Maggie stammered, "there were footsteps." She tapped a foot on the marble floor. "And then this Madeline, this live dead lady appeared—all—all—ghastly greenish white—and dripping blood—"

The three of them were out of the mausoleum in a rush, racing past tombs and cypress trees and some astonished visitors.

It was not until they were back at the boat landing that they stopped; gasping, and restraining hysterical laughter, they compared goose pimples. It was a draw.

Finally, Emilia said: "Oh, Maggie, that was beautiful! You think it is possible way back you have some Venetian blood in you?"

"Not that I ever heard of, but thank you for the compliment."

"And this poor Madeline, who was she? An ancestor?"

"Oh, no. She is a lady in the most creepy story I

ever read, 'The Fall of the House of Usher' by Edgar Allan Poe."

"Immediately, I must get it. Signor Poe, he is famous for his terrible tales. Signor Poe, he must have

had in him Venetian blood."

Still basking in the success of her terrible tale, Maggie did not argue.

It was the following afternoon, Wednesday, that the true adventure, as Maggie was to call it, began. Later she thought that if the Piazza of St. Mark hadn't left her breathless and in a weakened condition, it might not have happened.

The Piazza was one exclamation point after another. First, there was its size: enormous! an enormous beautiful outdoor *room!* Then there were the Basilica! the Moors on the clock tower! the *campanile!*

Dazed, Maggie allowed Emilia and Pietro to lead her down the immense length of the Piazza toward the Basilica. They went past tourists from all over the world snapping cameras, tourists old and young, hippie and straight, past postcard vendors, and strolling Venetians, some of whom greeted Emilia and Pietro. They went past pigeons, and pigeons went past them.

For once, Maggie was too dazed to keep an eye out for Vicky and Mike and Charlie.

In the late afternoon shadows, with hordes of people milling about and the tinkling of four outdoor orchestras, it was like a magical party. After Maggie had seen the Moors on the clock tower strike the hour and had sat astride the little red porphyry lions in the piazzetta behind the Basilica, which children have been doing since the early eighteenth century, they went to one of the grand outdoor cafés to have lemonades.

They found a small table, one of hundreds, and after some fussing to find a place under the table for her huge bag, Maggie sat straight and still and gazed around the Piazza.

While Emilia and Pietro had an argument as to which one of them would give the waiter the order for the lemonades (with a running interpretation by Emilia), Maggie went on with her gazing.

"Pietro does not understand that it isn't *just* because I am older that I should give the order, but that psychologically he no longer has to prove that he is a *man* just because he is a boy. Pietro does not understand the Women's Liberation." Emilia shook her head. "I think in Venice, it is going to be difficult, this liberation."

"Mm—" Maggie murmured, her attention elsewhere.

Cameras were snapping all around her. (One belonged to a professional photographer who solicited business by going from table to table.) But one photographer surprised her and held her attention. It was the Simenon man from the train. She saw him slip a tiny camera out of his jacket pocket, take aim, slip it back into his pocket as if it were a gun, and disappear in the crowd. All with amazing swiftness. And peculiar. What had he aimed at? Or *whom?*

Maggie was sure she had the answer in the next second. A familiar beard was rushing—elbowing his way—through the crowd. It was Mike, the hippie father—definitely rushing.

Maggie jumped up. And called out. "Hi! Mike!" Just like that. (Like some kind of nut? Without thinking? Or like someone looking for trouble?)

Then, regretting this wild impulse, she sat down. But it was too late. Mike stopped, wheeled around, and spotted Maggie. He hesitated. He looked behind him and over his shoulder. Then he walked slowly to the table. When he reached it, he gave Emilia and Pietro the once over with a sharp eye. They, in turn, regarded him with large, round eyes.

Maggie's heart pounded, and she was speechless.

"Like—you know—what are you doing in Venice—when you're supposed to be like in Cortina?"

"Because—because like my aunt is busted," Maggie stammered. "But—but what are *you* doing in Venice when you're—like—supposed to be in Trieste?"

"Well, man, like you know life is full of surprises—" he paused; then went on, more to himself, "like it sure is—and so like we're here—"

Emilia's elbows were on the table, and she was unabashedly making a serious study of Mike and this conversation.

As for this conversation, Maggie was certain it would not be taking place if Vicky had anything to say about it.

"Like are you kids all staying together?" Mike asked.

"No," Maggie said. "Like they're Venetians living in their own house."

"Oh, yeh, man."

Mike pulled on his scraggly newish beard, and one eye was screwed up as if he were trying to make up his mind about an important matter. The three children waited politely.

He finally addressed Maggie: "Man, how would you like to maybe make some bread?"

"*Bread?*" they all cried together.

"Here? In *Venice?*" Maggie was incredulous. Could there be an ordinary humdrum 4H Club or a Grange in this dream place? And if so, what would these hippies be doing with it? Or were Mike and Vicky in a commune?

"Sure, Venice. Just the place for bread. Why not?"

"I don't know. It seems like a funny thing to want to do in Venice. Don't you think so, Emilia?"

"We buy ours."

Mike hooted. "Man, like I thought you kids were hip to hip talk. Like bread is hip for you know money —the old buckaroo—lire—just what the man ordered when you're like busted."

The kids collapsed. "Oh-h-h!"

"So? What about it? Would you like to like make some?"

Be careful, Maggie warned herself. *This* could be dangerous.

"How?" she asked, cautiously.

"Baby-sitting with Charlie."

Maggie gulped.

"Oh." Dangerous, *very* dangerous, she reminded herself and played for time. "How is Charlie?"

"Fine. Man, he's just fine. You two really dug each

other. You ever baby-sit back home?"

"Uh. Well. Sometimes I have for our next door neighbor."

"I guess if you're old enough to make this trip alone, I guess you're like old enough to baby-sit. Maybe just for an hour or so. Maybe longer. So how about it? The usual rates like, of course?"

"Uh—"

Emilia gave her a big kick under the table, but its message escaped her. What was Emilia trying to tell her? Maggie ignored the kick and thought about the money. She and Aunt Yvonne could use some money. She was sure Aunt Yvonne wouldn't want her niece to get mixed up with hippies even if they weren't criminals, but a hippie baby couldn't be bad.

"Could Charlie come to my house? Like I don't think my aunt would let me go to—um—to a person she doesn't know."

Mike thought about this.

"As a matter of fact—like that might be--um—better . . ."

"When would you bring him?"

Mike pulled on his beard again. "Like—you know— I don't exactly know. You got a phone—man?"

"Like—yes. But it's awfully foreign . . ."

Emilia broke in: "If he calls, all you have to do is answer it, old thing, the way you do when I call. She's staying at Signora Cavelli's house—"

Mike grabbed a paper napkin from the table and jotted down the address.

"Now I gotta split. Like maybe I'll call you."

"Like okay," Maggie said.

Maggie watched Mike move swiftly through the crowd; move furtively, she thought.

"Wow!" she exclaimed. Feeling rather pale, she turned to Emilia and Pietro.

Emilia was resting her chin in her hands and was staring at Maggie intently. Pietro was play acting, pretending he was a hippie. He was acting crazy.

"Ignore him," Emilia said. "He is an exhibitionist. And you are an insecure person."

As if she needed to be told that. "I am?" Maggie asked in a small voice.

"Yes. Like—you know—imitating all that hippie talk. People who have to imitate other people are insecure. They need too much to be loved."

Maggie flushed. Well, there was *that*, but . . .

"Emilia, you may know all that psychology stuff, but when it comes to being a detective or—or an undercover agent, I'm the one who may know more about *that*. What about Mike's suddenly wanting me to baby-sit for Charlie? What about *that?*"

"What about it? Millions of people go in for that sort of thing, hiring people to sit with their children, don't they?"

"They don't go in for it so peculiarly. First they

absolutely ignore me. The mother hippie goes so far as to pretend not to know me. Now all of a sudden the father wants me to baby-sit." Maggie narrowed her eyes. "If you don't think the plot is thickening, I think you've got another think coming to you."

Emilia studied Maggie some more.

"I jolly well think you are living too rich a fantasy life. He looks like an ordinary hippie to me. I also think Signora Cavelli will not enjoy a hippie dirtying up her house. I think you could be thrown out. Do I have any more thinks coming to me?"

"No, thank you. Gosh! That would be awful, to be thrown out."

Emilia agreed. "It would be more mature in my opinion to say no, thank you to this hippie when he calls."

"You're the one who told him where I live," Maggie accused, crossly.

"That is true, and I regret it. It slipped out."

"But you may be right. Maybe if he calls I should say no. But it isn't only the mystery of it or the money. There is also Charlie. I happen to like him a lot. And I don't happen to feel like having him be kidnapped."

"You have a compulsion to be a heroine. It could be a dangerous compulsion. You are prepared for danger?"

Maggie decidedly felt a shiver up her spine.

"Mm . . . sort of . . ." Then she squealed. "Golly, why didn't I find out where *they're* staying? How could I be so dumb?" She banged her head.

"Because your name it is Maggie, not Maigret."

And neither is it Signor T, Maggie thought ruefully.

6

FROM THE MOMENT MAGGIE GOT BACK TO SIGNORA Cavelli's, she began to wait for Mike to telephone. At first, she had considered telling Signor T about this encounter immediately, but thought better of it: Wouldn't she be bothering a busy man with a piece of useless information? And as for alerting Aunt Yvonne to the *possibility* of Mike's call, why trouble trouble till trouble troubles you? Right?

Indeed, Maggie waited with a brew of contradictory feelings—excitement, curiosity, and some fear. What if her suspicions proved to be right, and Charlie really was a kidnapped baby? Was she really up to that much adventure?

That night, the Venetian night was filled with alarmingly foreign noises—bells, sirens, and a moaning wind. That night Maggie tossed restlessly.

However, in the morning the Venetian world was again tinted with its own lovely pale gold. And during the day, a swim at the Lido, a ride in Emilia's outboard motorboat, and a climb up the clock tower on the *Piazza* was so filled with wonder there was little time left for sleuthing and its troublesome problems.

Mike did not call that day and, exhausted by swimming, walking, climbing, and all that wonder, Maggie slept quietly and soundly that night.

Each morning, Maggie had watched the mail baskets being lowered from their window and the windows of the neighboring houses, had watched the mailman drop mail into them, had watched hopefully as Signora Cavelli pulled hers up. Even though Maggie knew that her mail had to be forwarded from Cortina, she had been disappointed.

At last, on Friday morning the basket was filled with treasure for her: a letter from her mother, a letter from her best friend Diane, a card from Mrs. Stone and, treasure of treasures, a letter from Jasper.

Maggie sprawled out on her bed. Jasper's letter

was set to one side to be opened last. Mrs. Stone's card was a view of the hill she lived on overlooking Nice and the Mediterranean. Her handwriting was spiky, like her. The card said:

Trust you too are collecting lovely memories. Am pleased to have collected you.

Yrs.,
Miranda Stone

Maggie smiled. Mrs. Stone was her first old lady friend and she was a great collector of lovely memories to have for future use. Mrs. Stone herself was a lovely memory to have.

Her mother's letter was motherly. It was well sprinkled with bits of hometown gossip, "darlings," "pets," worries, and lonesomeness for Maggie, and happiness at Maggie's good fortune in having this trip. It ended with a question:

Darling pet, have you had occasion to *need* your smile? Do not be afraid to tell me. I am not quite as hysterical as everyone thinks. Of course now that you are with your Aunt Yvonne, I feel (cross fingers and knock on wood) that you are safer. But do remember what I told you—you have a smile that could—if heaven forbid it were necessary—melt a heart of stone. I noticed it the

second you were born. Don't laugh. I did. Goodness, I do love you. And so does your father.
Even Sam does, no matter what he says.

Love,
Mother

P.S. Boy misses you, *too*.

Diane's letter was all about a horse she had gotten
for her very own. Its name was Velvet after guess
who. (Did that stickler for facts and figures remember that Velvet was the girl, not the horse? Ha!)
Naturally, it was the most beautiful, the most intelli-
gent horse in the world. And it was also a cinch to
ride. And loving. Which would Maggie rather have
—a horse of her very own or some trip to Italy?

A *horse?* For one terrible second, Maggie could
have kicked beautiful, exquisite Venice in the teeth.
Or was it by some chance—Diane?

Before opening Jasper's letter, Maggie jumped off
the bed and gave her hair a brisk brushing.

Jasper's letter began with "Hi." Just "Hi." Not
"Dear Maggie," or anything like that. And it was
magical the way that "Hi" brought back their early
mornings in the bow of the ship when they were all
alone watching for whales, porpoises, and flying fish.
That "Hi" brought back the start of their lifelong
friendship.

"Your olfactible letter," Jasper wrote,

has been tested with my olfactometer (I busted my dictionary on this one), and I am happy to report that while the smell of salami was present, *no* trace of baloney (sic) was detected. In plain English, kiddo, I dig you and your suspicions about those hippies. For one thing, you're not all that easy to hate on *first* sight. On the other hand, remember that hippies make a big thing about being peculiar. And about those sticks Charlie was playing with. My guess is they were I Ching sticks. Hippies are into I Ching and tell their fortunes with the sticks. Think I'll try some of that stuff myself. To be honest, my own future does interest me.

About fantastic. I agree with you. What do you think about dwimmery? A dwimmer is middle English for wizard. (See *The Hobbit*.) Doesn't dwimmery sound like dreamy with a lisp and sort of . . . fantastic?

Jasper warned her to be careful about playing detective in a foreign country, but signed the letter,

Yours for more and more dwimmery adventures.

Dwimmerly yours,
Jasper

"Dwimmerly, dwimmerly, dwimmerly yours . . ."
Maggie was singing when the phone rang in Signora
Cavelli's quarters.

It was for Maggie, and it caused mass hysteria.
Signora Cavelli flew to Aunt Yvonne with the alarm-
ing news that a *man* wished to talk to the *bambina*.
Should it be permitted? Aunt Yvonne thought *not*.
The child did not know any *man*.

"Who can he *be?*" Aunt Yvonne moaned from
the imprisonment of her chaise.

"Only a father who wants me to baby-sit," Maggie shouted, sprinting toward the phone.

"No, *no*, NO!" Aunt Yvonne cried, grabbing for
her crutch.

"*Please—*" Maggie begged.

"I forbid it."

"Oh, please, Aunt Yvonne, Charlie will be brought
here."

"Who in heaven's name is Charlie?"

Maggie started jumping up and down, which she
hadn't done since she left home.

"The baby, the baby. He'll hang up. And that'll
be the *end* of it. Oh, *please!*" Maggie reached high C.

Aunt Yvonne covered her ears. "Tell that man to
call back in a half hour."

Maggie ran to the phone thinking aunts were
possibly worse than mothers.

"Man, what took you so long to get to the phone?

Like are you living in the Doge's Palace?" Mike was annoyed.

"Could you—would you mind calling back in—in fifteen minutes? I've got to explain things to my aunt."

Mike didn't answer. Then she could hear him whispering, probably to Vicky. Then there was silence. "Are you there? Are you there?" Maggie asked frantically.

"Yeh, I'm here. But like if there's any problem about your aunt—"

"Oh, no. She just doesn't know about how *every-one* baby-sits back home. I'm sure it's going to be okay—"

"Well—like try and explain it in ten minutes, will you? It isn't like you know you have to explain the second law of thermodynamics."

"I'll try," Maggie said, but thought, I'll bet it's harder than that, whatever that is.

"Tell her Charlie wouldn't hurt a fly."

"I'll tell her."

It took twelve minutes and Maggie using that smile of hers for all she was worth to convince Aunt Yvonne that baby-sitting was an honorable **profes-sion**, that making money *was* for children, that she knew *how* to baby-sit having done it a million, trillion times before (an exaggeration), and that Charlie wouldn't hurt a fly let alone Siegfried.

"But what about Signora Cavelli?" Aunt Yvonne worried. "You know how she is."

"Charlie's a very good, little baby. He won't bother her."

Maggie saw no reason to confuse matters by describing Charlie or Charlie's parents.

Aunt Yvonne finally agreed, but reluctantly and mournfully. "Nothing is turning out the way I planned it. Between that wretched debenture and that naughty Siegfried, here you are . . . somehow to be *baby*-sitting in Venice . . . *Venice* where Tintoretto, Tiepolo, and Titian painted . . . How long will this Charles person be here? And what will he eat? And what will you *do* with him?" Aunt Yvonne's black eye was fading to violet, matching the color of her eyes, which were now fluttering. "A *baby!* Good God!" She leaned over and spoke to Siegfried. "Siegfried, a baby! It isn't my fault, darling, and do please behave, *please?* For my sake?" She dropped her voice to a whisper, "He can be very jealous."

As Maggie ran from the room before Aunt Yvonne could change her mind, Aunt Yvonne called after her: "What about the canals . . . ? What if the baby . . . ?"

A soft moan wafting from the chaise chilled the back of Maggie's neck. What *was* she letting herself in for? And why?

The hippies arrived to the sound of bells ringing all over Venice and in the distance the boom of the cannon going off in San Marco. All this to celebrate the noon hour.

If the ooze of the lagoon had suddenly seeped into her house, Signora Cavelli could not have been more violently affected by the arrival of the hippies. Her eyes bugged; she paled; she trembled; and she wrinkled her nose—and all but held it—as if they stank like bad fish.

Maggie thought it the rudest exhibition she had ever seen and felt sorry for the hippies even if they were kidnappers.

Besides, come to think of it, this hippie chick smelled like Aunt Yvonne, very expensive. Wasn't that peculiar for a chick?

For their part, the hippies were too busy trying to refold the small portable carriage they had wheeled Charlie over in to notice Signora Cavelli's distaste. The carriage had obviously just been bought in Venice. Charlie, clutching his sticks, looked around the dark hall with large, solemn eyes, let his eyes rest for one alarmed second on Signora Cavelli, and then toddled to Maggie with a flashing smile.

With the carriage finally folded up, Vicky turned to Maggie and said, nervously: "Like—you've baby-sat before?"

"Oh, yes."

"Fed it?"

"Of course."

"Changed it?"

"*Sure.*"

"You wouldn't let Charlie fall into a canal—like would you?"

"Sure. I mean, of course not. I'm awfully reliable when it comes to babies."

"And—like it's okay with your aunt?"

"Oh, sure."

"Well like—okay. Here's Charlie's . . . grub bag. We don't know how long it's going to be you know. We may be back in a couple of hours . . . maybe longer. But if you take Charlie for a walk, don't go far. And don't get lost. And there's a banana and some cheese and zwieback and a thermos of milk. And if he gets sleepy, like his security blanket's in the bag and a change of pants and . . . like . . . you know . . ."

At this point, Vicky took notice of Signora Cavelli, who was standing with her arms akimbo regarding Charlie, who was drooling on a stick, with undiluted distaste.

Vicky spoke to Mike: "Like if Charlie isn't welcome here?"

"Charlie *is* welcome. Isn't he, Maggie?"

Maggie scowled at Signora Cavelli. Then she leaned over and hugged Charlie. "You bet he is."

But Vicky was not convinced.

"Like—?"

"Like come along and like stop being a mother," Mike scolded.

"But—"

Vicky went to Charlie and gave him a kiss and a hug, which he squirmed out of and which Maggie considered excessively intense for a separation of a couple of hours.

"Mind you keep your eyes on Charlie," Vicky admonished as Mike began to shove her out the door.

She isn't fooling me, Maggie thought, anyone can *act* like a mother, even a hippie can.

As Maggie walked Charlie up the stairs, slowly, carefully, step by step, she thought that with these peculiarities adding up, she had better begin to list them. In a pretty little notebook. She loved pretty little notebooks and used any excuse to buy them. At home she had little notebooks used for listing RESOLUTIONS ABOUT FRIENDSHIP, CONFESSIONS, RESOLUTIONS ABOUT IMPROVING MYSELF, PET HATES, and other private matters. They had been left under lock and key in her toy chest, away from Sam's prying. The book she would now buy in Venice would be called PECULIAR CLUES. The prospect of owning a *foreign* notebook with a title like that so excited her that she began to hoist Charlie up the steps two at a time.

Charlie's meeting with Aunt Yvonne and Siegfried did not go well. At sight of Charlie's raggedy jeans and dirt-streaked face, Aunt Yvonne tried to smile kindly while hiding her fright.

"Oh . . . ah . . . oh . . ." was all she could say.

Siegfried, on the other hand, was openly hostile. He growled.

Which made Charlie howl. Violently.

Which made Aunt Yvonne lunge to grab Siegfried, almost breaking her good leg in the process.

"Out . . . out . . ." Aunt Yvonne gasped, hanging on to the squirming, still growling Siegfried.

Using all her strength, Maggie lifted Charlie from

the floor and tottered out of the room, clutching Charlie around his middle. Once in her own room, they both collapsed on the floor.

"Poor . . . poor darling Siegfried," Maggie heard. "Naughty darling, there's no need to be jealous." Then, louder: "No need to be jealous at all."

Maggie crawled to the door and closed it.

Charlie was still howling, his feet kicking Signora Cavelli's frayed, but pretty, rug. Maggie bore down on the feet.

"Char-lie, *please* stop, oh, *please!* If Signora Cavelli hears you . . . Oh, *please!* I am your friend, *friend,* Charlie, and I am going to help you, help you, Charlie, really and truly I am."

Charlie still howled.

Maggie's hand slipped off one foot, the foot shot up and clouted her under the chin.

"Ouch!" she yelled.

Charlie stopped howling and watched with great interest as Maggie rubbed her chin.

"Kiss . . ." he said.

Maggie stopped rubbing her chin. "Kiss?"

"Kiss . . ." Charlie repeated.

So hippie mothers kissed hippie babies' bumps just like regular mothers. Or . . . did they?

Maggie made a mental note to mark this down as another peculiar clue. She also could not help flattering herself that, like Maigret and Signor T, she was beginning to pay a lot of attention to human behavior.

Charlie sighed, shuddering as he did so. And he stuck his thumb in his mouth.

"Poor Charlie," Maggie whispered. "Charlie—who is your real mommy?"

Charlie sighed again.

Maggie decided his security blanket was in order.

The inside of the grub bag was surprisingly neat. The food was neatly wrapped, and Charlie's changes of pants were surprisingly white, bleached as white as babies' pants in Tilton, Iowa.

Maggie pulled out the security blanket—blue, luxuriously soft, and *clean*. Then she saw a gleam of silver at the bottom of the bag and reached for it. It was a silver case, about the size of a business card, and engraved in an old-fashioned way. It was also beaten up and, examining it closely, she saw teeth marks, undoubtedly Charlie's. That wasn't too surprising, because she had a locket she had teethed on, too.

But what if there was a clue in this little silver case? Her locket had pictures of her mother and father as children. The detective in her needed to know. She gave Charlie his security blanket, which he promptly stuck in his mouth, while she tried to find out. The case wouldn't open. Charlie had done a fine job of jamming it. Finally, with the aid of her scissors—and a jab that brought blood—Maggie pried the case open.

It contained a picture of Charlie, a much-cared-for Charlie, in the arms of a lady who was smiling dotingly down on him. A square Charlie with a square lady in a velvet chair.

Maggie's heart flipflopped sickeningly.

She stared at the picture long and hard. The lady was young, prettyish and stylishly dressed, silky *rich* stylish, like a lady who could pay a big fat ransom if she had to.

Maggie crawled over to Charlie and held the picture up in front of him.

"Mommy? . . ." she whispered.

Charlie reached for the case.

But Maggie wasn't ready to give it to him.

"Mommy? . . ." she coaxed, pointing to the picture.

"Mommy, mommy, mommy," Charlie gurgled.

Maggie knew enough about babies to know that Charlie could be playing a game.

"Daddy . . . ?" she tried.

"Daddy, daddy, daddy," Charlie gurgled.

"Oh, Charlie!" Maggie cried impatiently.

Maggie stared at the picture again, imploring it to give up its secret. She stared at Charlie; she pushed back his hair. Was there a resemblance between him and this lady? Yes, there was a decided resemblance. If the lady was Charlie's real mother, then Charlie was a real kidnapped baby. Her heart, still flipflopping, tried to deny it but her eyes confirmed it.

And she, Maggie, was . . . what? A born detective? Maybe even a real heroine?

Or a real scared, little girl?

7

MAGGIE SAT STILL, CLINGING TO THE SOLID SAFETY OF the floor. She gazed at the unsafety of the case in her hand; she gazed at Charlie. Poor Charlie. Poor kidnapped Charlie. It must be scary to be a kidnapped baby. Never mind that Charlie was sucking peacefully at his security blanket, even gurgling. Inside of him, he must be lonely for his real mommy, his real daddy, maybe some real brothers and sisters, maybe a real dog who wouldn't growl at him. Poor, darling Charlie must be saved. And without a minute to lose.

Then, into this pity for poor little Charlie there crept a note of envy. Kidnapped or not, right now it was a cinch to be a baby compared to a heroine who had to *act*. Truthfully, this heroine was all at once overwhelmed by a desire to curl up next to Charlie and clutch at another corner of his security blanket. Truthfully, she simply felt too young for this much adventure.

But Venetian bells were ringing, warning that time was passing and that she had better act before it was too late, before Mike and Vicky returned, took Charlie with them, and disappeared forever.

Maggie knew that she must get hold of Signor T. But that involved getting Signora Cavelli's help with the phone, Venice to get lost in, and Charlie on her hands.

There was, of course, Aunt Yvonne, right out there on the other side of the door. But past experience with grown-ups warned Maggie that Aunt Yvonne wasn't going to believe that Charlie was a kidnapped baby. "It's just your vivid imagination, darling," or "Too many whodunits," or "Something you ate," is what she would hear. And with Aunt Yvonne's tendency to get hysterical, she might break another leg. Besides, if she, Maggie, had to go off to find Signor T, she could not leave Charlie here with an aunt with a broken ankle, a dog ready to chew him to bits, and the unfriendly Signora Cavelli ready to throw him into a canal.

The person she needed was Emilia. Emilia could

phone Signor T and Emilia could take care of Charlie.

Charlie, exhausted from his howling, was half asleep as Maggie tiptoed out of the room.

Siegfried, exhausted, was lying across Aunt Yvonne's stomach. Aunt Yvonne was also exhausted.

"I'm sorry, Aunt Yvonne."

"That's all right, darling. Siegfried is naughty, such a little snob. You see, he likes babies to be clean. Why is this one so—well *not* clean?"

Maggie's back stiffened. "Because he happens to be a hippie baby, Aunt Yvonne." Maggie made that sound as royal as possible.

"*Hippie?* Good Lord! I didn't know they went in for having babies. Hippie or not, don't you think he ought to be washed up a bit?"

"Uh-uh. He'd start to howl again. What I thought I'd do is take him for a walk with Emilia."

Aunt Yvonne brightened perceptively. "A splendid idea. And Maggie, darling . . . about baby-sitting. I think it's really not done here. You know, it may be just a little bit provincial? Baby-sitting? And since one of the purposes of this trip is . . . ?"

Fixing Aunt Yvonne's bad eye, Maggie said, with cool innocence, "Okay, Aunt Yvonne, when in Venice I'll try to do like the Venetians do."

"*Like . . . ?*" Aunt Yvonne murmured, pained.

Maggie could barely restrain her laughter, hysterical laughter. Here she was embroiled, yes *embroiled* in an international crime and this grown-up was worrying about being *provincial* and *grammar*. Typical.

Signora Cavelli came in, scowled at Maggie, and let loose with a furious torrent of Italian.

"*Si, si, si,*" Aunt Yvonne raised her hands in truce. She spoke softly in Italian. Then she said to Maggie: "I have apologized to Signora Cavelli. I have told her that it was all a mistake, that it will never happen again, that from now on babies are forbidden. I said you were a perfectly lovely, little girl who wouldn't dream of causing anyone trouble. Isn't that true, darling?"

"Well, I wouldn't *dream* of it . . ."

Aunt Yvonne raised a warning eyebrow. "Mm— I'm sure Signora Cavelli would be charmed by a sincere, little apology?"

"I apologize sincerely, Signora Cavelli." Maggie spoke as if she had marbles in her mouth.

Signora Cavelli grunted.

"Signora Cavelli, now could you please get Emilia on the phone for me?"

When Signora Cavelli learned that the phone call would remove the dirty baby from the house, for a while at least, she flew to the phone.

"Emilia—?"

"Oh, Maggie. I was about to telephone you. It would be jolly beautiful today to go again to the vault at San Michele. Beautiful and cloudy. A perfect day for terrible tales, this time my tales. You would care for this?"

"I can't. I have the baby. Can you meet me at the bridge?" Although Signora Cavelli was no longer standing by, Maggie still dropped her voice. "It's fearfully important."

"Oh. Is it about—?"

"Shh!"

"But we are alone. Pietro and I. No one is here to hear."

"Even so. You never can tell. Will you meet me right away? *Please?*"

"Righto."

It took muscle and patience to get the drowsy, lumpish Charlie down the stairs and into the stroller.

Aunt Yvonne had hobbled to the top of the stairs to watch.

"Darling, you will be careful about the canals, won't you?" she called down.

"Uh-huh."

"And you will be back before they return, won't you?"

"I think so."

"*Think* so?"

"I mean if they come back too soon—I mean *sooner* —tell them I took Charlie for a walk."

"Oh, please do see that you're back. I don't know

how to talk to hippies, all that awful language."

"Okay, okay."

The beautiful cloudiness of Venice was oppressive and gloomy, warning of a storm on its way.

As she pushed Charlie toward the bridge, Maggie suddenly worried about running into Mike and Vicky, and kept seeing them in every approaching hippie. If that should happen, there would be no possibility of fleeing with the baby in the carriage.

Maggie began to sweat.

Emilia and Pietro came toward her.

"Ba-by," Pietro said.

"No, no," Emilia scolded. "Do not call him a baby. It could . . ."

"Never mind all that psychology stuff. I've got something to tell you, and I need your help."

As people stared curiously at the three children walking the dirty little hippie baby, Maggie told her tale of the snapshot that proved Charlie was kidnapped.

At last Emilia was satisfactorily convinced: she gasped; and for once Pietro did not do a cartwheel: he too gasped.

"What is it you wish of me?" Emilia asked, none too eagerly.

"If I give you a number would you get it for me?"

"Whose number?"

"I promised not to tell. But this kind of business is his business." Maggie knew her face was a perfect study of someone giving away a secret while keeping it.

"Oh. Oh, Madonna! I know who that is. Pietro told me about that adventure. He's the man from—"

"Shh!"

"He *too* is in Venice?"

Maggie nodded.

"Madonna! Is not this Venice remarkable?"

"Yes, yes. But will you or won't you?"

"You are sure it is all right to bother such an important man?"

"Emilia!" Maggie stamped her foot.

"Very well. I will do no more than to get the number. You must understand that my parents are very strict and it is forbidden for me to get mixed up with American crime. Also Pietro's parents."

Having seen Pietro's parents on the ship, Maggie knew Emilia was right about that.

"Is there a public phone around here that's very private?" Maggie asked.

Emilia didn't know; she had never before been faced with this problem. However . . . thinking it over, she said that since everyone was gone for the day, they could use the phone at her house. It would be private, and it would also save lire.

Maggie had been to Emilia and Pietro's house once

before during her week in Venice. That time, it had
been by way of the canals. Emilia was allowed to use
an outboard motorboat, and after taking Maggie on
a sightseeing tour of the canals, they had ended up at
Emilia's house for lunch. Now, taking turns pushing
Charlie, they went in and out of alleys, over several
little bridges, through an arch formed by a building

that straddled a street, and across a square. It was a bewildering route that ended in a darkish alley where the houses were all secretively shuttered. Here, in the cloudy heaviness, the air seemed particularly thick with gloom.

Inside all was highly polished and satiny, not frayed like Signora Cavelli's house. "We will use Pietro's phone. But do watch Charlie," Emilia warned. "Both our mamas have phobias about dirt. They would have to be tranquilized if they saw Charlie. It is not just our mamas however. Venetian babies are the most clean in the world, you know."

Although Maggie was distracted by the urgency of the situation, she still flared patriotically: "The babies of Tilton are mighty spotless, too. Don't forget that Charlie is incognito. Aren't you, Charlie?"

But Charlie was taking in another strange house, and his eyes were glazing.

Maggie dug out Signor T's scrap of paper.

"Here. I guess it's all right now if you know that you call him Signor T. It will be easier and quicker if you ask for him."

None too happily, Emilia went to the phone. She spoke rapidly in Italian, then stopped and covered the mouthpiece: "She sounded suspicious, but she's going to see if he's in his room." There was a long wait, then: "*Si?* Oh, *si, si, si.*" Emilia spoke to Maggie: "He's not there, but he should be back in about an hour. What do you want me to say?"

"Golly! I don't know. Can he call here?"

Emilia shook her head emphatically. "I told you our parents forbid mixings with crime or scandal. It is absolutely forbidden. You better go back to your place and have him call you there." Into the phone, she said: "*Si, si.*" To Maggie: "Hurry. You must decide . . ."

"Okay, okay. My aunt isn't exactly wild about crime either, but tell him to call me there. Say it's terribly urgent."

By the time Emilia hung up, Maggie had her plan worked out.

"Okay. I'll go back to the house. But I'd better go alone, so you keep Charlie here."

"Are you insane? We can't do that."

"Emilia! Do you want to save this baby or don't you?"

Emilia seemed not to know.

Maggie knelt down next to Charlie and put her cheek next to his. "Poor, darling Charlie . . ."

"Stop that. You will give him a persecution complex . . ." Emilia lowered her voice. "He's so d-i-r-t-y. Our parents—"

"Now look who's giving him a complex. All right, Charlie, we'll leave, and if you aren't saved, guess whose fault it will be. We Americans may be loaded with crime and we may not be as hoity-toity as you

Venetians, but we are mighty kind to babies and we are used to risking our lives for them."

"Except when you kidnap them." Emilia spoke to Pietro who answered with a raised fist. "Pietro says we Venetians are more kind to babies, that our parents are not here, and suggests that we can somewhat wash Charlie. Pietro is a true Venetian, practical. We will keep Charlie, but not too long. Hurry back as fast as you can."

"Back? Golly, I'll have all I can do to find my way home. And back, too?"

"Pietro will take you to the bridge, and on the way give yourself landmarks to remember."

Maggie gave Emilia instructions in the care and feeding of Charlie, gave Charlie a hug and a kiss, and took off with Pietro.

Following Pietro, who ran more than he walked, back through the alleys and over the bridges and under the building, Maggie would make him stop while she tried to fix a facade or a wellhead or a stone animal in her head. In vain, she thought. Getting back alone to Charlie would be like trying to find her way home in a nightmare. She wished that she could leave a trail of crumbs like Hansel and Gretel.

Pietro left her at the *Accademia* Bridge and went whistling off. For a second or two, Maggie stood and watched him as he ran, winding in and out of people who were strolling, dawdling, or going briskly about their Venetian business unaware that a major crime was taking place. She had an impulse to race after Pietro and get back to Charlie. Charlie was her charge, and she ought not to have let him out of her sight. After all she had been engaged as a baby-sitter, not a detective.

She rejected that impulse, however, and went on her way overloaded with worry and guilt.

8

THE FIRST SIGN OF SERIOUS TROUBLE WAS SIGNORA Cavelli leaning out the window, scowling, clearly on the lookout. When she spotted Maggie, she became agitated and waved to her to hurry, hurry.

Maggie ran as fast as she could. Oh, Lord, she thought, the hippies have returned and done something *awful*. Or Aunt Yvonne has broken her other leg. Or Emilia called to say something terrible has happened to Charlie, that he fell into a canal. Or—

Signora Cavelli had the door open.

"The baby, where is it the baby?" Signora Cavelli shrieked.

So Mike and Vicky had returned.

"I'm not saying. Where are they?"

"You *not saying?*" Signora Cavelli raised a hand as if she were about to smack Maggie. Then, more menacing, the hand pointed up the stairs. "Upstairs—"

Ignoring Signora Cavelli's command to hurry, hurry, Maggie dragged herself up the stairs.

Real life adventure didn't play fair. At least she should have been able to talk to Signor T first, gotten some instructions. Suppose, for instance, they were armed? Real life adventure was turning into a real life nightmare.

She heard Aunt Yvonne's voice, at its most dramatic, strangled: "Maggie—? Maggie, darling—?"

For all she knew they were holding a gun to Aunt Yvonne's head. Such things happen in real life.

"*Maggie?*"

"Com-ing—" Her voice was strangled, too.

Whatever happened, Charlie must be saved. She supposed.

At the top of the stairs Siegfried waited. His nose was pointed upward, indignantly.

Maggie leaned down and patted him. "Be friendly. Please. To me."

At the entrance to Aunt Yvonne's room, Maggie stood still.

It was not the hippies who were waiting for her. Two men were standing across the room from Aunt

Yvonne, standing poised to pounce.

"Maggie?" Aunt Yvonne looked completely distraught.

"Charles? Where is Charles?" the taller of the two men demanded. He had a pale, round face and pale, colorless eyes, and he was wearing a black silk summer suit. What could a black silk suit have in common with Charlie?

Maggie didn't answer. Her eyes rolled toward the second man. And opened wide with recognition.

134

This man was the Simenon man. He smiled, but not nicely.

"Where is it the baby?" he asked with ghastly softness.

Maggie went over to Aunt Yvonne. All at once the realization that Aunt Yvonne was her own flesh and blood became a shield.

"Who are these people, Aunt Yvonne?"

"That is what I would like to know. I don't know who they are. I don't know what they're doing here. It's the most upsetting and bewildering . . . Who are you—sirs?"

"Madam, I have already told you. I am the boy's father." The man in the silk suit jabbed his thumb into his chest. "And I have come to get him. There is nothing confusing about it."

"*You* are the father?" Maggie was not quite as surprised as she pretended.

"He is the father," Simenon assured her.

"The *real* father." Silk Suit added.

"Maggie—do you know what this is all about?"

"Um—no." Maggie's knees were beginning to wobble.

"Gentlemen, kindly identify yourselves. I believe that it is only proper that you do so." With considerable effort, Aunt Yvonne was pulling herself together.

"The *signora* is right, *signor*. The *signor* is Signor

Bruce Mason, an American businessman. And I—I am myself Ferrari." Simenon bowed.

Aunt Yvonne blinked. "Yes, of course. But some identification, if you please? Passport? License? You know, something?"

"The *signora* is right, *signor*." Ferrari took out his wallet and presented a business card. "I, too, like that all should be proper."

Grudgingly, Mr. Mason presented a passport.

"My glasses, darling." Having won this point, Aunt Yvonne was becoming languid.

"Where are they?"

"Oh—let me think—"

"Madam!" Mr. Mason exploded. "You are driving me crazy!"

"That, sir, is your problem. I never do know where they are."

"She can read, can't she?" He pointed to Maggie.

Maggie took the card and the passport. All this time she had been only half listening. Mostly she had been busy thinking.

"It *says* Ferrari, and it *says* Mason, but—"

"But nothing. Where is my baby? What have you done with him?" Mr. Mason's pale voice was pitched unpleasantly high. He came toward Maggie.

"*Signor*—if I may be so bold—it is for a professional to make the inquiry, yes?" Ferrari put out a restraining hand. "Signorina Maggie, I am Ferrari, the detec-

136

tive. I am the one who followed the hippies from Milan. Yes? And it is I who followed them here. Yes? And I know they left with you the baby. Yes? So now, Signorina Maggie, it will be wise to tell us where is the baby. Is not that so?"

"No, that is not so."

"Maggie, darling!"

"How am I supposed to know this—this person *is* Charlie's father? The passport only says he's Mr. Mason. There's not a word about his being Charlie's father."

"Ah, a clever child," Ferrari said.

"That *was* clever of you, darling."

"Of course I'm his father. What else would I be? Here are my—" He pulled out his wallet again. "My credit cards, my American Express, my license—"

To her surprise, watching Mr. Mason lose his cool quieted Maggie.

"What have those got to do with Charlie?"

Mr. Mason began to get blustery.

"Time is short. Make her tell," he ordered Ferrari.

"The child wants more proof. Clever, clever . . . *Signor*, you have the proof?"

Mr. Mason's pale face turned mauve.

"Damn it. What was I supposed to travel with? his birth certificate?"

"A picture perhaps? The family in group?"

"Carrying family pictures is not my style." He

attempted a smile. "Maggie—that is your name, isn't it?"

Maggie was feeling stronger and stronger: holding the secret of Charlie's whereabouts was a powerful weapon.

"Maybe it is and maybe it isn't."

"It is so your name," Mr. Mason yelled. Making an effort to control himself, he went on: "Now, I understand that you're being cautious, and I must say I appreciate your caution. It is an admirable trait. But my dear child, time is of the utmost. Any minute it can be too late. There is no point in keeping it a secret from you—my son Charles has been kidnapped, and I have traveled three thousand miles to recover him, and recover him I shall!"

"*Kidnapped?*" Aunt Yvonne was horrified. "Oh, why wasn't I firm? I knew baby-sitting wasn't right! *Kidnapped?*"

"I knew it all along," Maggie said.

"You *what?*"

Maggie patted Aunt Yvonne as if to say, "Please keep out of this and let me handle it." "Where is Charlie's mother?" Maggie asked Mr. Mason. "The lady in the locket?"

Mr. Mason regarded Maggie as if he could not believe his eyes: This flea was pretending to be an elephant?

"The lady in the locket? That's not his mother,

that's his aunt."

"Then who *is* his mother?"

Before he could answer, the bell downstairs rang. They could hear the excited voice of Signora Cavelli: "No *bambino!*" Then feet racing up the stairs.

The hippies rushed into the room, wild-eyed. They didn't seem at all surprised to see Mr. Mason and Ferrari.

"Charlie! Where's Charlie?" Vicky cried.

"Don't say!" Mr. Mason shouted and clamped his hand over Maggie's mouth.

Aunt Yvonne screamed. Siegfried yelped. Maggie bit Mr. Mason's hand. Mr. Mason cursed.

Ferrari lit a cigarette.

Mr. Mason sucked on his hand, then said to Ferrari: "Call the police. Have these people arrested. All of them!"

"Arrest?" Aunt Yvonne had grabbed a crutch. "No one is arresting my niece. She is an absolutely innocent child. Aren't you, darling?"

Hooray for flesh and blood! Maggie thought.

"Uh-huh."

Ferrari puffed on his cigarette. "That remains to be seen. So—where is he, the baby?"

"Yes—oh yes, where is my baby?" Vicky was weeping.

Mike leaped to Maggie's side. "Whisper it in my ear."

Mr. Mason screamed at Ferrari. "Do something you—"

Ferrari's cigarette was now in the center of his mouth, and he was puffing away as he considered the matter.

"Is difficult when is child what is accomplice."

"Accomplice?" Maggie moaned.

"Ah-h-h," Ferrari crowed.

Vicky came close. She had quieted down. "She is not an accomplice. She is Charlie's friend. Aren't you?"

"Yes I am." Maggie looked around at these people towering over her, examined each one from top to toe. "Maybe the best friend he has in the whole world. And I am not going to tell where Charlie is until you all tell me who you are."

"Bravo, darling, bravo," said Aunt Yvonne.

"I am his father," Mr. Mason snarled. "And *she* is a kidnapper." He pointed a trembling finger at Vicky. "And so is *he*." He pointed at Mike. "And I am getting my son back from these filthy hippies."

"*I* am Charlie's mother, and I am not a filthy hippie, and I hate this wig." With which Vicky tore at her hair, gave it a yank, and pulled the wig off. Her own hair was short, blond, and freshly shampooed.

"And *I* am Charlie's stepfather, and I am a businessman."

Aunt Yvonne cocked her head at Mike. "Sir, I do

hope you don't mind my asking but—is yours a wig, too?"

"Yes it is, and I feel like a fool in it—"

"Then—why not . . . ?" Aunt Yvonne twirled her fingers in the air.

"Excellent idea," Mike said, and yanked his wig off.

This was too much for Maggie: she laughed hysterically.

"Stop this vaudeville show!" Mr. Mason bellowed.

"Stop being a louse!" Mike bellowed back.

Ferrari rocked on his heels.

"I am not a louse. I am exercising my legal rights, my duty as a father. Under no circumstances was Charles to leave the United States without my permission. Those were the terms of the divorce papers. And you know it."

"But Mike had to come here on business. And you knew *that*. Why couldn't you have given permission? You—you—"

"Why should I? And why did you have to come along? What kind of mother turns herself into a hippie? turns *my* son into a hippie just to go off with *that* hippie? There's enough evidence here for me to get full custody of Charles, and I intend to do just that."

"No, no, no," Vicky cried. "You can't do that. Mike needed me here with him. I know Italy and I know some Italian and he doesn't. I've got to help him get started, set up appointments . . . Just this morning, he needed me to help him look up stuff at the library. We weren't going to be gone forever. Just for a few months. Any decent person would have said yes. You just said no to be mean. You're always mean, always. You forced me to do this. For all I know, this is just what you wanted to happen so you could get Charlie away from me . . ."

"Charles could have stayed with me while you were gone."

"For months? Alone in that house while you go off to your precious office?"

"Of course not alone. With Mrs. Adams."

"*That* witch?"

"That witch is an excellent housekeeper who wouldn't have turned my son into a hippie."

"Don't be ridiculous. That was only a disguise, and you know it. Besides, Charlie likes it."

"That's *your* story. You have broken the agreement set down by the court. You have broken the law. You are not a fit mother. Charles is going home with me, and he is going to stay with me. And that's that."

Vicky began to weep again. Mike went to her side and put his arms around her.

"Now, young lady, where is my son? No more excuses. You know the whole story. Quickly!"

Ferrari walked toward Maggie. He meant business.

"Quickly!" he repeated.

"Uh—"

"*Si—?*"

"Yes?" Mr. Mason snapped his fingers.

Vicky and Mike watched anxiously.

"Come on, come on," Mr. Mason ordered.

"I hate you!"

It had just popped out. But having popped out, this truth was beginning to have an interesting effect: an idea was taking shape.

"Well, I can't say I'm crazy about you either. But what's that got to do with law and order? Law and order, young lady, that's what this is all about."

"No, it isn't. It's about Charlie. I don't think Charlie wants to go home with you."

"Says who?"

"Says me."

Mr. Mason addressed Aunt Yvonne.

"You'd better order your niece to cooperate. Instantly. Or *you* will be an accomplice too, madam."

As Aunt Yvonne's good eye iced, the lavender one narrowed, giving her a sinister and somewhat disreputable look.

"I don't find you to my taste either," Aunt Yvonne said, with a haughty wave of dismissal.

Vicky's face was drawn to a white mask and her eyes turned watchfully. Mike was pulling his straggly beard.

Mr. Mason turned on Ferrari. "Don't stand there, you idiot! Do something!"

Ferrari pursed his lips.

"Why *can't* Charlie stay here with his own mother if he gets all cleaned up again?" Maggie asked.

"Because—because the agreement says—"

"I don't care what the agreement says. I won't tell where Charlie is until you say that he can stay here with his mother. Until you write it down. And that you promise not to try to get that full—full custody. So there."

Vicky and Mike grabbed each other's hands. Aunt Yvonne gazed at her niece with amazement and pride.

Mr. Mason was livid. "Why you little—" His hand shot out.

Ferrari tapped Mr. Mason.

"Signor. Let us to consider. For myself, I congratulate Signorina Maggie. She holds now the best card. In the game of life who holds the best card wins. Sometimes. Come to the corner, signor, and let us to consider, you, signor, and me."

Grudgingly, Mr. Mason went to a corner of the large room with Ferrari.

Vicky and Mike, looking very much like a pair of paper dolls in their hippie clothes and their straight hairdos, were straining to catch what the other two were up to. Unfortunately, the room was too large for eavesdropping or lipreading.

Aunt Yvonne beckoned to Maggie to come close. She whispered: "Darling, the theater's in your blood. You're splendid. An excellent Portia. Goodness! And this is Venice! Oh, what a divine charade!"

The compliment pleased Maggie, but at this moment the role of detective took precedence over that of Portia. "Do you think they're up to tricks?" she whispered. "Did you hear him say '*sometimes wins*'?"

"Yes. Watch your step."

In the corner, it was Ferrari who was doing the talking. Mr. Mason was shaking his head. Then Ferrari said something that stopped Mr. Mason's head from shaking. Mr. Mason frowned, pouted, and finally nodded.

They marched back, side by side.

Mr. Mason said: "I have decided to sign this ridiculous agreement—on one condition." It was Maggie he addressed.

"Which is?" Maggie asked.

"That I am to see Charles with my own eyes, safe and sound, before I go."

Mike looked up, surprised. "Sure. Why not? With us standing by that is."

Mr. Mason glowered at him. "Okay. Let's get this nonsense over with and get to Charles."

Maggie produced a pad and a pen and handed them to Mike. Mike hesitated: "Me? I'm supposed to write it? I'm no lawyer."

Maggie was sure Mike knew better than she did, how to say it, but . . .

"Just say that *he*," she jabbed a finger in Mr. Mason's direction, "promises on his word of honor that Charlie can stay here with you and Vicky and that he won't do that business about trying to get Charlie away from Vicky for keeps. And then he signs his name and you keep the paper, and that's all there is to it. I think." She would have liked to ask for a drop of blood on the paper, but she didn't think these grown-ups would understand about that.

"Portia, Portia—" Aunt Yvonne crowed.

"Ridiculous, ridiculous to be blackmailed by a child." Struck by a new idea, Mr. Mason shouted at Vicky: "What kind of a baby-sitter was this to pick for *my* son?"

More than a little dazed, Vicky replied: "An incredibly competent one it seems."

Mr. Mason sputtered angrily.

Mike finished writing and handed him the paper. He put his glasses on and examined it, word by word. He handed the paper to Ferrari who also examined it word by word, mouthing each one. Shrugging, he handed it back to Mr. Mason.

"Blackmail!" Mr. Mason snapped, as he signed the paper, which Mike plucked out of his hand before he could change his mind.

"I don't like the way he's saying 'blackmail' so much," Vicky said. "If you're up to any tricks—"

146

"Now look here, I just signed the paper and I don't want any more discussion. Where's Charles? That's the agreement."

With everyone's eyes on her, Maggie could not resist a dramatic pause.

"Well?" Mr. Mason shouted.

"You don't have to shout at me that way. I'm going to tell you. Charlie's safe and sound at my friend Emilia's house."

"Who's Emilia?" Vicky asked.

"Who's Emilia? This is a fine time to be asking that question." Mr. Mason shook his finger at Vicky. "A *good* mother—"

"That's enough of that," Mike interrupted. "Where does this Emilia live, Maggie?"

"Uh—" Maggie reached for her bag which was on the floor. "Not too far from here. Just over some bridges and through some alleys . . ." She sat down on the floor and began the usual hunt through the bag. Nervously.

"Oh, my God!" Mr. Mason was beside himself. "I have a plane to catch!"

Maggie found her notebook and held it up triumphantly. "If someone will call Emilia, she'll bring Charlie right to the *Accademia* Bridge. That would be the fastest way, wouldn't it?" And relieve her of the need to be the guide, if that should prove necessary.

Surprisingly, for once without further argument,

this plan was accepted by all concerned. Ferrari was the logical one to place the call, but they all followed him and Maggie to the phone.

Ferrari gave the operator the number. They waited. And they waited some more. Ferrari turned to Maggie.

"There is no answer?" he asked incredulously.

Vicky caught her breath.

"Take it easy," Mike urged her.

"Keep on trying," Maggie urged Ferrari. "It's a big house."

"My God!" Mr. Mason banged the wall.

They waited silently while Ferrari tried again. He hung up. "This is the correct number?"

"We've always gotten her on this number before. Oh! Emilia's probably in Pietro's apartment, and I don't have that number."

Mr. Mason banged the wall again.

"But I know where the house is. I think."

"You think?" Ferrari was very quiet. "But you have the address, yes?"

Maggie sighed with relief. "Yes, I do."

"Please?" Ferrari held out his hand.

Maggie handed him the open notebook. He studied it. He squinted.

"This number. The first one. This is a two or a three, please?"

Maggie studied the number. "It's a—it's a—it's a

three. Of course."

She handed the notebook back to Ferrari. He looked at the address with pursed lips. He looked at Maggie. He spoke sternly: "In Venice, the difference between a one, or a two, or a three, it can be the difference between the beginning or the end of a district, a matter of much streets, canals, bridges, and alleys. In Venice, they do not number the way they do in the rest of the world. Myself, I have the good fortune to come from Milan. And now it is my hope that we have the good fortune for you to know your numbers. For my taste, it is not a three, it is a two." There was a murmur from the others, and he held up his hand. "We will take the *signorina*'s word. *Andiamo!*" He motioned them to come along. "And also you know the house, is it not so?"

"Yes sir," Maggie said with a slight quaver. "Please, I must say goodbye to my aunt and tell her where we're going."

"Make it snappy," Mr. Mason ordered.

Aunt Yvonne was putting on lipstick. "I always face up to a crisis better, darling, if I'm all put together," she explained apologetically. "Now do tell me—"

Maggie told her.

"Oh. Oh, how I wish I could go with you. You will remember to tell me everything, won't you? And darling—please do promise to be careful."

Maggie promised.

"And Maggie—I am proud of you. That father may be the real father, but he'd never get custody of Siegfried, not for one minute. I believe you have saved that poor baby from that hateful . . ."

Maggie kissed her hastily. As she ran from the room, Aunt Yvonne called after her: "Darling, you know besides being a Portia, you're also a Solomon. It's too wonderful."

Signora Cavelli didn't agree. She shooed them all out with her arms waving wildly, as if they were an infestation of locusts to be gotten rid of.

Indeed they were an odd-looking troupe. Setting out close to a trot, Maggie and Ferrari were in the lead. At their heels, Vicky and Mike, nine-tenths hippie and one-tenth straight, blocked Mr. Mason from forging ahead of them. The darkening sky had emptied the streets, but there were still many who turned to stare.

After they left the *Accademia* Bridge, Maggie began to check her landmarks. She did remember that house with the arched windows and the lace curtain flapping out of one window. The breeze had ominously died down and the curtain was now limp. A wellhead seemed familiar. But it was a lion that began to unsettle her. Surely she would have noticed how sad it was? and that it was walleyed?

What if that number had been a two?

After all Venice must be filled with houses with arched windows and lace curtains hanging out and walleyed lions.

Maggie began to pray.

Ferrari, without any hesitation but beginning to pant, kept on going over the bridges, under the arches, through the alleys. Maggie was no longer paying attention. He was a big, grown-up detective who knew where he was going. She hoped.

When he came to a little alley, he stopped, looked up at the numbers, and led them to the house.

Ferrari knocked. Ferrari rang. There was no answer. Instinctively, they all looked up: the house was shuttered. But Venice was a place of shuttered houses, and *all* the houses on this little alley were shuttered.

Ferrari banged on the door, rang again. There was still no answer.

He turned to Maggie: "This alley . . . it is the right one?"

Maggie looked around wildly. Like the rest of Venice, this alley had also darkened. Stone houses, stone animals, balconies, shuttered windows—so many alleys, so many canals, so many bridges, this beautiful Venice, this beautiful city to be totally lost in.

"Please to answer—"

"I—I can't."

Maggie began to panic.

9

MR. MASON COULD BARELY TALK. "IS THIS—OR IS THIS not where you left my son? If this is a trick, I'll—"

Maggie dropped her eyes. A great babyish howl was gathering in her throat and had to be held back at all cost. She raised her eyes. Was this or was this not Emilia's house? In the sunless, storm-blackened light, the stones of this house were gray. Had Emilia's been pinkish or yellowish? And if this was Emilia's house, where *was* Emilia? *Charlie?*

"Maggie! Oh! Oh! Mike!" Vicky's panic stabbed through the heavy air.

Mike spoke quietly: "If everyone keeps calm, it'll

help. Let's see the notebook, Maggie."

It was fished out with the usual complications.

Mike studied it. "Maggie, once again, is this a two or a three?" There was a decided edge to his voice.

And the voice of Miss Jensen, math, echoed through the Venetian alley, thundering doom: "Make your numbers legible. One sloppy illegible number can cause a disaster. A *dis–aster!* Never forget *that!*"

Oh, Miss Jensen, I did forget.

Maggie's eyes blurred with tears. "I—I still think it's a three. That is, it looks like a three to me."

"She *thinks.*" Mr. Mason snarled at Vicky. "You turned my son over to this—to this nincompoop. You irresponsible coldhearted *hippie!*"

Mike sprang at him. Vicky screamed. A shutter flew open on the ground floor of the house next door, and a woman stuck her head out and called out in Italian.

Ferrari answered her. Then he said to them: "I will find out from her about this house and who are the people."

He went over to the woman and got into a low-keyed conversation with her. When he came back, his mouth was pursed.

"It is the right house."

Maggie sighed with relief. Mike patted her on the shoulder.

"But—" Ferrari paused dramatically, and spoke

directly to Mr. Mason, "but it is to regret to say that these people they do not have the first-class reputation—"

Vicky, Mike, and Mr. Mason all spoke at once: "What is that supposed to mean?"

Ferrari shrugged: "Perhaps it is only gossip that the woman speaks. She mentions a certain nastiness with the government about lire. But you know how it is with neighbors, the truth may be elsewhere, such as a quarrel over a cup of flour. On the other hand— one must accept the possibility that these people had suddenly to flee—"

"The police! The police! Get the police!" Vicky implored.

Mike tried to calm her; Mr. Mason growled at her; Ferrari tried to silence them all.

In the hubbub Maggie tried to tell them that Emilia and Pietro's parents seemed very respectable to her and that Emilia had said they were very strict about crime, but that anyway she knew just the person to get to find them. No one would listen to her.

When Ferrari had silenced them, he said: "This is not yet for the police. It is for me to take over. Alone. Absolutely alone. It is recommended that you all go to café around the corner and wait while I pursue the investigation."

"But—" Mr. Mason protested.

"*Signor!* It is recommended *highly*." Ferrari pierced

Mr. Mason with his eyes.

"What do you think?" Vicky asked Mike.

"Wait how long?" Mike asked Ferrari.

"It is impossible to say. But I have the confidence that *quietly*, *calmly*, without the emotions, understandable as they are and also natural, I will recover for you the baby. Give me first one hour."

"Well—okay," Mike said slowly, "but I warn you —both of you—that if I get impatient, I'm calling the police."

"*You're* calling the police? Let me remind you that my son, Charles, is in Italy illegally."

"And let me remind you that you just signed a paper, witnessed—"

"Bosh! Rubbish! Under the circumstances—"

"Oh, please," Vicky broke in, "let's just get Charlie back. That's all I care about now. Come on."

Ferrari, with Mr. Mason beside him, led the way. Holding hands, Vicky and Mike followed. Maggie walked alone. This was a quiet little corner of Venice and in the sultry, prestorm tension only two cats were out with them.

All at once, beautiful Venice was a sinister place and this was all surely happening in a nightmare, the sort that at home would send her crawling into bed with her mother.

They came out on a small square, and the outdoor café was empty, which added to the nightmarishness.

A waiter bustled out to greet them. His eyes took in their number, and he picked a table that would hold them, first dusting it off with a napkin. Mr. Mason took a step toward another, smaller table, then thought better of it. Ferrari called out to the waiter who had poked his head out from under the awning to look at the weather. The waiter shook his head, then indicated that they should still try the outdoor table.

Maggie looked up at the sky, too. She now knew that there was nothing so lost as a lost baby. Now she understood those hysterical mothers of lost children at the fairs back home. With every second that was passing, she was feeling Charlie's lostness more painfully, more guiltily. But for Charlie to be lost in the midst of a huge storm would be too much.

Like four characters in a silent movie, they took their places at the table. Mr. Mason scraped his chair as far away from them as he could.

Ferrari told them to wait for him, that he would be back within the hour. With Charlie. He had his sources, he assured Vicky with bravado.

The three grown-ups had *espressos* and Maggie tried to get a lemonade down and couldn't. No one spoke. Mike and Mr. Mason kept glancing at their watches. Vicky kept looking at the sky. And Maggie didn't know which way to look.

She was beginning to hate everyone who had sent her on this trip to Italy; most of all she was beginning to hate adventure; she wished she had stayed scared.

Presently, Mr. Mason rose and said: "I am going to telephone my hotel. I've been waiting for an important business call."

After he left, Mike took Vicky's hand. "It's going to be all right." He didn't exactly radiate confidence.

"Why don't we call the police?" Vicky asked.

"We will if Charlie isn't back in an hour."

"An hour is an eternity. Anything can happen in an hour."

Maggie swallowed. "It's all my fault. I left Charlie with Emilia because I was sure you were kidnappers (which you sort of are, she almost said), and I wanted to get Signor T to work on it."

"Signor T?" Vicky and Mike asked together.

"He's a— Oh, I'm not supposed to say who he is. But I can tell you this, if anyone can find Charlie, he can."

Mike and Vicky looked at Maggie dubiously.

"He could too—" Maggie muttered under her breath.

Mr. Mason returned. What remained of his coffee was cold. He ordered more. He lit a cigarette. He snuffed it out. He looked at his watch, scowled at it as if time were passing without orders from him.

"Perhaps we ought to call the police after all—"

"Are you losing confidence in your man?" Mike asked.

Mr. Mason tapped a finger on the table. Maggie

thought he was the most fidgety man she had ever seen. "He was highly recommended for cases like this and—and he did keep his tail on you—"

"You—you idiot." Vicky spoke bitterly. "If you hadn't put a detective on our tail . . . and a clumsy one at that . . . we wouldn't have gone in for all this hippie stuff and . . . Charlie wouldn't now be, now be . . . oh, where?"

"You don't have to rub it in." Mr. Mason was unexpectedly contrite. "I want him back as much as you do."

The first faint rumble of thunder was to be heard in the distance, ricocheting over the tile roofs, the domes of churches, coming in from the mainland of Italy.

"Are Venetian storms bad?" Vicky asked.

Neither Mike nor Mr. Mason knew.

Maggie squinted up at the sky. In Tilton, Iowa, those huge thunderclouds, along with this smothering heat, meant a big storm was coming. Maggie kept this weather wisdom to herself.

Once again, they stopped talking.

About three-quarters of the endless hour had passed when the waiter came out and said Mr. Mason was wanted on the phone. Vicky, Mike, and Maggie started. Mr. Mason shook his head. "It's not about Charles. Because of that business call I'm expecting, I left this number at the hotel."

He was gone for just a few minutes.

"I have to return to the hotel. A call from the States is coming in for me. I won't be gone long. Just long enough to return the call. Ten minutes at the most. Will you wait here with Charles—or without him?"

Vicky and Mike exchanged looks.

"Okay," Mike said. "It is the only decent thing to do, I suppose."

"*Decent?*" Mr. Mason was contemptuous. "Yes, that would be decent. To be allowed to see my own son before I fly home."

He strode off like a man who would not allow himself to be lost in Venice.

"A business call!" Vicky said. "At a time like this! And he wants full custody of my Charlie."

Mike smiled weakly. "I'll say one thing for both of us, honey. Your taste in husbands has improved."

Vicky tried to smile, too.

Venetian bells, muffled in the heavy air, rang.

"Hour's up," Mike announced.

Vicky's eyes widened with fear. "Well, where is he? that detective?"

"Vicky—the man said *about* an hour."

"Should I go back to Emilia's house?" Maggie asked. Sitting still was becoming unbearable.

"What for?" Mike asked.

"I don't know. Maybe Emilia and Pietro have

come back. Maybe Emilia just took Charlie to the cemetery . . . Maybe . . ." She had already gotten up.

"Okay. But come right back, will you? Or soon we'll all be chasing each other all over Venice."

She ran off. Between the heat and her enormous bag, running was hard work. However, when she saw Emilia and Pietro leaning against the front of the house, she picked up speed. When they saw her, they ran to meet her, bursting with excitement.

"He's saved! He's saved!" Emilia cried. "Charlie he is saved!"

Pietro did a cartwheel.

"Where is he?" Maggie gasped, struggling for breath. "Where's Charlie?"

Emilia waved her hand toward the farther end of the alley.

"He took him. The detective did."

10

WITHOUT STOPPING TO THINK OR WONDER AT THE UN-
likeliness of it, Maggie cried: "Signor T!"

"Signor T? No, no, Signor Ferrari."

"*Who?*"

"Ferrari. He showed me his card," Emilia said,
proudly.

"Oh! Oh-oh-oh! How long ago was it?"

"Perhaps a half hour or so. What is the matter?
What is it?"

I am now about to get hysterical, Maggie told herself. Then to confirm it, she clutched her head and
let out an ear splitting screech.

"Shh! Are you going mad?"

Maggie stopped screeching and groaned. "Yes. I am. It was a trick. They've grabbed Charlie. The telephone calls were tricks. You went and gave Charlie to the enemy. Oh—" Another screech was on its way.

"Stop that! I did no such thing. He is the detective of the *real* father." She pointed to the house next door. "Signora Albani she said it was true. The father, the hippies, *you*, she saw you all together."

"I am going to kill myself. Dead, dead, dead. How am I going to tell Vicky? She will kill me, too."

"But I don't understand."

"That *signora* next door told him your family had a bad reputation, that you all had to flee."

"*My family?* Signora Albani told him no such thing. He is a big, bad liar. My family is an old and a proud family. It is one of the best in Venice. I tell you we do not flee. My family will kill him."

"But where *did* you go?"

"To my grandmother's. My grandmother, she had need of her fish poacher, which my mother had—"

"*Fish poacher?* You gave Charlie back to his rotten stinking father because of a stupid old fish poacher, whatever that is?" Maggie's face was screwed up in agonized disbelief.

"In Venice, when our grandmothers order, we obey. In Venice, we do not keep fish until it stinks.

In Venice—" Emilia began to weep. "I wish I had never met you. The boat, it got the trouble. Was not then Charlie kidnapped?"

"Yes and no. I wish I had never met you, too. I wish Jasper were here. He would know what to do."

Emilia sniffled. "So he is not here, this Jasper. But your Signor T, he is. Is he not?"

Maggie clutched her head again. "Why am I standing here like an idiot?" She picked up her bag.

Still sniffling, Emilia said: "Because you had the traumatic—"

"Come on. Let's go. We'll tell Vicky and Mike—" They raced back to the café.

At sight of the three children racing toward them, both Vicky and Mike jumped up, knocking over their chairs. The scene that then took place seemed irrationally affected by the gathering storm. Vicky seemed to have gone into shock, Mike seemed about to hit everyone in sight, Emilia and Maggie seemed about to weep themselves sick. And Pietro, standing off to one side, seemed to be enjoying the excitement.

The waiter and the patron came out to see what was going on.

"The hotel. Quick! to the hotel! Why are we standing here like lumps?" Vicky began to move.

"Which hotel?" Mike's voice was frighteningly hushed.

Of course no one knew. There were the grand

luxe, the luxe, the very comfortable, the good and comfortable . . . Emilia started to name them—the Gritti, the Danielli . . . No one was listening.

"Signor T, Signor T . . ." Maggie droned. No one listened to her either.

"The police! I want the police!" Vicky shrieked.

"And they'll want *you*," Mike said. "Vicky, I hate to remind you, but Charlie isn't supposed to be here, not legally."

"He is so supposed to be here with his mother. I don't care what anyone says. I want Charlie—"

With which Vicky howled like a little girl.

This triggered Maggie into shrieking: "And I don't care what anyone says either, I'm calling Signor T!"

"Who the devil is that?" Mike asked.

"I promised I wouldn't tell. But I can tell you this —if anyone can get Charlie back, he can. He's famous for getting valuable things back. *Please? Please*, Mike? I love Charlie, too. And I don't want him to go with that ratty father."

Mike studied Maggie. "You're sure he's okay, Maggie? on the level?"

"On my honor. Cross my heart." Maggie crossed her heart.

"There's nothing to lose," Mike said to Vicky, who was now weeping softly.

"Except time. Every second counts."

"Well—that's true, but—but call him, Maggie. It

may be too late, but—"

Maggie fished out Signor T's address. "If Emilia will get the number, I'll talk to him. That is, if he's there."

Emilia, enjoying her importance, found the way to the phone. They all trailed after her.

While Emilia made the call, Maggie crossed her fingers so tightly they hurt.

Signor T was in.

"Here—" Emilia handed Maggie the phone.

Maggie thought the pounding would burst her heart as she waited for Signor T.

"Yes?" Signor T sounded coldly anonymous, rather bored.

"This is Maggie."

"Ah, my friend the adventuress. I returned your call, but you were not there." He was indulgently reproachful.

"I know. Because I'm here. Because everything's happened and it's awful. We need you to do something *immediately*."

There was a soft chuckle.

"And where is here? And what is it that has happened? And what is it that is awful?" The indulgent tone still prevailed.

Maggie sensed that once again she was up against the stone wall of grown-up disbelief.

"Listen—" she began to plead when the phone was snatched from her.

Vicky took over. "I don't know who you are, but my baby is gone. I'm the mother. Level with me. Oh, please, can you or can't you help? The child says you can. Every second counts. I'm desperate!"

Apparently, that got through to Signor T.

Vicky went on: "Kidnapped—about a half hour ago—um yes—you see—what? oh—" She turned to them. "Where are we?" Emilia took over and told Signor T. She handed the phone back to Vicky. "He wants to talk to you." "But—*wait?*" Vicky cried. "I tell you every second counts. Oh! Well okay—okay—"

She hung up slowly. "He says this isn't for the phone, that we should wait here, that he'll be here within ten minutes."

"*Ten minutes?*" Mike shouted. "By that time, Charlie can be out of Venice. If he's not already . . ." There was a crash of thunder. "Well maybe not by plane."

"He said if Charlie wasn't already out of Venice—" Vicky caught her breath. "He said no baby was going to be leaving Venice as of now. Oh, Mike, what do you think? Should we wait?"

"How did he sound? reliable?"

"How should I know?"

"I know," Maggie said. "He is so reliable. Please believe me."

"Well—the point is what would we do if we didn't wait here? We don't want to go to the police, we

167

don't know where to begin to look. Let's wait for a while anyway."

And they began to wait, without talking, and without once looking at each other. Even Pietro seemed to have lost his appetite for excitement, although he couldn't keep still: he watched his feet toe in and out endlessly.

As for Maggie, slumped in a chair as far as she could go without sliding off, she knew she was going to spend the rest of her life with this squirmy wormy feeling inside her from having ruined little Charlie's life. Not to mention her own.

Outside, the patron and the waiter moved the tables close to the building and turned them upside down to protect them from the storm.

The first rain began to fall as Signor T appeared, walking daintily under a huge umbrella, walking as if time was his special possession.

Hurry, hurry, hurry, Maggie screamed furiously —and silently.

Signor T did not hurry. He shook the few drops of rain off his umbrella before closing it. He furled it tenderly, running his hand over each fold to press out any potential wrinkle. He appeared unmindful of people waiting for him with nerves frazzled to the snapping point. More than that, he appeared unaware of them, period.

Therefore it came as a shock when he said: "Maggie if it is the life of adventure you are determined to lead, you must stop the nail-biting or you will be like the *Venus de Melos*—without the arms." But, by the time he had stopped fussing with his umbrella, she had stopped chewing on her nails.

And then he spoke a word or two of Italian to Emilia and Pietro, having determined their nationality—by what? their clothes? their noses?

The biggest surprises were reserved for Vicky and Mike.

"Ah, signora and signor, your disguises, they were not foolproof. Signor, your sandaled left foot, it shows it was too recently set free from a shoe one size too narrow." They all stared at the tiny red bulge on Mike's little toe. "And *signora*—not only, of course, the label, which you neglected to remove—in your overexcited state of course—there is also every sign that the jeans were prematurely, artificially rumpled, not ripened by nature. In particular, those wrinkles there. Tsk-tsk. Disguises are not easy." He bowed. "Forgive me."

Maggie could see that in spite of their frantic impatience, Vicky and Mike were impressed: this man was a highly skilled, professional observer. He also, it became obvious, was a professional questioner. In a matter of minutes he had extracted *their* story.

"And so," Mike concluded, "my wife was helping me this morning. It was foolish I know, but we thought Charlie would be safe with Maggie. We did not notice that we were being followed that time."

Signor T had listened attentively, but did he believe them?

All of them, even Pietro, stared at Signor T with faces strained with anxiety. They waited.

He asked to see the paper Mr. Mason had signed. He studied it. He looked at Maggie quizzically.

"Portia . . ." he murmured.

"I will keep this for the moment?" he asked Mike.

"Uh—of course."

He spoke to Emilia in Italian. She shrugged and said, "*Non so.*"

"I asked her what was the fish her grandmother wished to poach, and she does not know. I am very fond of poached fish. Whenever I am in France I eat it. In Italy we do not poach, we boil. I am impressed that her grandmother owns a fish poacher—"

"Oh, my Lord—" Vicky wailed, "this man's talking about fish when Charlie may be . . . What are we waiting for?"

"A telephone call, *signora.*" Signor T took a heavy gold watch out of his vest pocket. "Any minute now."

"Are you going to help us?" Mike asked. Mike struggled to be courteous, but the implication was— "Or aren't you?"

Signor T's face remained fat and smooth and

utterly without expression.

"The father, he has a legal right to the child, is it not so? And your wife, she had not the right to take the child out of the United States, is not that so?"

Vicky and Mike didn't answer.

"The father is a rotten, stinky, awful, terrible stuffed shirt," Maggie blurted out, "and I hate him and so does Charlie."

"You know that for a fact?" Signor T asked.

"Well—uh—well, he will if he has to live with him for the rest of his life."

This exchange was interrupted by the patron who came over to say that Signor T was wanted on the phone. At that moment, the storm broke overhead. They all moved to the doorway to watch it. Maggie had seen much worse storms, fierce midwestern ones with hailstones as big as tennis balls, but they had been like the violent temper tantrums of a relative or an old friend—familiar and usually predictable. This one crashing and spilling over Iowa would have been humdrum; over Venice, it was terrifying and also too beautiful for any word but dwimmery.

Signor T joined them. He squinted at the blackened sky ripped open with streaks of lightning.

"The plane—it should take off ten minutes after the storm has passed over the airport. We ought not to hold it up too long. So *andiamo!* The *motoscafo* it waits for us."

Pietro was about to do a cartwheel, but Signor T shook his head.

"Only the principals must come."

Pietro and Emilia's faces fell.

"What about me?" Maggie asked.

"Ah, but you are a principal, if not *the* principal."

"But I'm the one who gave the baby to the man," Emilia protested.

"For that you do not get the medal of honor. However, later you may be a principal, too. *Avanti—avanti—*"

Maggie waggled fingers at Emilia and Pietro. They didn't waggle back. They were furious.

Vicky was already out in the rain. Signor T raised his umbrella over her. Signor T didn't run, but he

moved with incredible speed. Mike and Maggie followed, drenched to their skins.

Maggie was impressed with the importance of being a principal. Also the danger. One could easily be struck by this dwimmery lightning. "Who *told* you to be a principal?" she could hear her mother ask hysterically; her mother, who was just normally hysterical, went clear out of her mind about people out in an electrical storm.

The *motoscafo* bobbed up and down in the churning little canal. Only barely visible through the rain-streaked window of the cabin, a man was gesturing. Shaking his head and waving his hands, he was refusing to drive them in this storm.

But Signor T ignored him and leaped onto the boat. He held his hand out to Vicky.

They crowded into the cabin. A few words from Signor T, spoken softly, and the protesting boatman gave in. They took off.

They left the small canal for the Grand Canal. There, the boatman let the throttle out as far as it would go and they planed over the water as if they were flying. But at least, Maggie could see, there was no danger of a collision because scarcely anyone else was crazy enough to be out in the storm. Maggie knelt on the bench and pressed close to the glass. Behind the rain and the gloom the palaces floated, imaginary and dwimmery. When lightning streaked across one pink palace in particular, that palace, Maggie thought, could never have had a more beautiful moment and would remain one of her memories, collected forever.

"But you *are* going to help us, aren't you?" Vicky asked Signor T again.

"*Signora*, I make no promises. I have now only your story."

Making a sharp turn, sharp enough to tilt them toward each other, they left the Grand Canal and cut through another small one leading to the lagoon.

Entering the lagoon, the full force of the wind whirling in from the Adriatic hit them. The little boat tumbled about, shuddered, and lost speed.

Maggie shivered. This was the lagoon of Emilia's taletelling, a watery phantasmagoria of ancient enemies gruesomely defeated, criminals whose punishment was to be drowned here, ghosts, legends—and boats getting stuck in its shallows maybe forever.

"The *laguna morta*—" Signor T announced.

The lagoon of the dead. Rising ghostlike from it, that would be San Michele, the cemetery, Signor T found it necessary to tell them.

Maggie wished she had a hand to hold.

Signor T spoke to the boatman.

"What did you say to him?" Mike asked.

"I told him to watch his *bricole*—those sticks out there that mark the channels. To be stuck now would be disaster. We must get to the canal that leads to the airport."

As if on cue, there was a sickening crunching under the boat.

The boatman shouted.

Signor T translated: "Everyone to one side!"

They obeyed silently.

The boatman rushed from the wheel, and Signor T replaced him.

On the open deck, in the drenching rain, the boatman picked up a pole and began to shove. The propeller churned furiously, but the boat did not budge. Signor T cut the motor. The silence was terrifying.

Signor T spoke to Mike: "Youth before age? a small push?"

"Oh—of course—"

"But Mike is not a good swimmer—" Vicky protested.

Mike was already out of the cabin.

"*Signora*, if it was necessary the swimming, there would not be the problem. It is the shallowness that is the problem. The man did not watch the *bricole* well enough."

"Now will we lose him? Will Charlie be gone?" Maggie whispered to Signor T.

Signor T did not answer. He had one hand on the throttle and his head was bent as he listened intently.

The storm was receding, leaving them in a vast

and lonely quiet. The only noises to be heard were ugly: the gurgling of the mud and a crunching that could very well be the bones of Emilia's hordes of corpses.

It was in her toes that Maggie felt the first faint sliding. Simultaneously, Signor T opened the throttle to the lowest speed. Maggie kept her eyes on the pole the boatman was pushing against the mud. Little by little, its slant increased as the boat slid away.

Maggie let out a squeal of delight. The boat was afloat.

The boatman pulled the pole out of the mud; Mike scrambled aboard with wet and muddy legs; and Signor T gave the throttle the gun.

They were on their way again.

11

THE BOAT SCUDDED OVER THE LAGOON LIKE A DE-mented water creature. This time they all kept a tense watch as the boatman navigated the *bricole*.

The rain was reduced to a drizzle, and when they flew past a fishing smack, Maggie could see the fishermen stare at this crazy *motoscafo*.

By the time they reached the airport, the rain had completely stopped and a man in uniform was waiting impatiently for them.

"Please to hurry—" he said. He held out a hand to Vicky, who needed no such urging. She was the first to leap off the boat.

"Which way?" Vicky asked.

In the distance, Maggie could see a plane with the steps hooked to it, ready for passengers.

But the man pointed to the administration building. With Vicky leading, they all began to run, except Signor T. As usual he did not run, but skated swiftly, gracefully, mysteriously.

Mr. Mason, Ferrari, and Charlie were in an office off the main lounge. If frustrated rage could make a man burst apart like an overblown balloon, Mr. Mason was about to do so. On the other hand, Ferrari looked like a player in the game, May I? who was not sure of the move. And Charlie? Charlie, whose face had been washed and whose hair had been brushed, was spread-eagled in his stroller. He was grinding his teeth in the troubled sleep of a baby who's had it.

Vicky ran toward him. Mr. Mason tried to block her. She shoved him aside and dropped down beside Charlie. Not wanting to wake him, she hugged herself as she gazed at him adoringly.

"What is the meaning of this?" Mr. Mason snarled. "The Italian government will hear about this outrage, holding up a whole plane—"

"Yes, *signor*, by all means," Signor T purred.

"And who the devil are you?"

Ferrari lit a cigarette.

Signor T identified himself.

Ferrari took a long, slow pull on his cigarette.

Mr. Mason shifted from a snarling man to a suavely injured one. He bowed: "Um—ah—yes. In point of fact, sir, I am relieved to have your assistance. This baby—this poor baby—my son—was illegally—surreptitiously—taken out of the United States by this—by these people, and I have come three thousand miles, three thousand miles, sir, to take my son back with me, back where he legally belongs."

"You have the proof, *signor?*"

"Proof? Proof of what?"

"That it is with you the *bambino* belongs, *signor.*"

Watching Mr. Mason struggle for composure while coming out in violet patches, Maggie almost felt sorry for him.

"Ah—um—if you mean the custody papers, they are in the vault in the bank at home. Where they are safe. Naturally, that's where they are."

"Naturally? I have a different opinion, *signor.* I would say more natural would have been to bring proof with you."

The violet patches were deepening to purple.

"Sir! One—the bank was closed over the weekend and I could not risk waiting until it was open. And two—I did not expect to have a—a—" he glared at Maggie "a mere child butt in and complicate matters. Sir, I am the father, my son properly belongs with me when his mother goes gallivanting all over Italy.

If I may say so, these people should all be in jail."

"Including the child who butts in?"

"Well—uh—"

"Signor—" Signor T reached into his pocket and brought out the paper. "Signor, this is your signature?"

Mr. Mason tried to laugh suavely, but the best he could do was more like a hysterical giggle.

"*That?* That was a piece of nonsense that this child thought up. Sir, I played along in order to find my son." Mr. Mason drew himself up. "In order to *save* my son from—from I didn't know what since he had disappeared. And from these disreputable, irresponsible, lawbreaking people. Surely, sir, that is understandable? And surely, sir, this silly piece of paper dictated by a child is not legal?"

Signor T gazed at the paper.

"I am not a lawyer. The courts here—"

At this point, the man in uniform said: "Please, signor, the plane. Our schedule—"

"*Si, si,* you are right." Then, Signor T continued: "*Signor,* it is your right to test this in the courts. You send for the custody papers, the mother presents this paper, in a matter of some weeks—"

Maggie's heart began to sink. Papers? Courts? Poor Charlie.

Charlie stirred, as if he had been listening to all this in his sleep.

Mr. Mason stopped trying to be suave.

"Weeks?" he shouted. "Papers? Courts? *Italian* courts? Sir, I am an American businessman. *American*. I have business at home. Important business. I want to see the American consul. Immediately. I will not be denied my rights as an American citizen!"

Everyone started to shout. Vicky, who left her watch over Charlie. Mike. The man in uniform. Ferrari who had been mute. Everyone except Signor T, Maggie, and Charlie.

Maggie was watching Charlie wake up.

She tugged at Signor T's jacket. Then she whispered into his ear. He listened attentively.

"Silence!" Signor T ordered. He had barely raised his voice, but it carried like a silent dog whistle: they obeyed him.

"*Signor*, the plane it must go. The baby he must stay until there is proof. It is my duty, signor, to suggest to you that should it come to a judge to make the final decision, in Italy there is a predisposition to decide in favor of the mother. In Italy, the mother she is sacred. Unless—unless it should happen that the child in question shows more love for the father. So— in order not to waste your so valuable time, *signor*, it is proposed we make a trial test now. We let the baby to give a hint. Let us see which it is he wishes to be with—the mother or the father. *Si?*"

"No! This is more nonsense!"

"Yes, I agree nonsense. However, in these matters where the babies are concerned, the heart it often rules the head. So it is from such nonsense that decisions are—how shall I say? nudged? But I can see that you do not trust this nonsense? that you feel it will not be in your favor?"

"Nonsense! I mean Charles is very fond of me—"

"He is not!" Vicky blazed. "It's Mike he adores—"

The man in uniform wrung his hands: "The plane it cannot be held up for a popularity contest! Please!"

"*Signor?* You stay? You go?" Signor T inquired.

Mr. Mason walked over to Charlie. He walked like a man with a gun in his back. He knelt down beside Charlie.

Vicky leaped to the other side.

"Charles?" Mr. Mason's smile was the most forced Maggie had ever seen.

Charlie looked at his father with cool disinterest.

"Charlie? darling?" Vicky held her arms out.

Charlie looked at her coolly, too.

"Charlie!" Vicky coaxed.

Charlie looked up and around at everyone watching him as if they were watching a missile about to blast off. Then he smiled broadly and held his arms out. Grunted to be picked up.

By Maggie.

Signor T laughed. Mike laughed. Vicky laughed. Mr. Mason did not laugh. He stood up. "I told you

182

it was nonsense. Look here, I can't fool around any longer with all this—this Italian nonsense. I've got a big deal pending." He spoke to Vicky. "I'm going to let you get away with it this time, but I warn you—"

Signor T stopped laughing. "And I warn you, *signor*, that in Italy we care for legal matters to be settled in the courts, not by taking the law into your own hands by *kidnapping—kidnapping, signor*. It is only because I too have to leave Venice that I do not hold you here on that charge. So—there will be an end to nonsense and next time your former wife she has to come to Italy on legitimate business, I suggest to you to cooperate. My message, you get it?"

The mighty fell with a big flop. Mr. Mason became embarrassingly meek. "Yes—yes, sir."

Ferrari had busied himself gathering Mr. Mason's dispatch case, bag, coat, and umbrella. He opened the door and kept his eyes carefully fixed on the plane to be seen in the distance, waiting.

Mr. Mason gathered the tattered remnants of his dignity, hesitated for a second before giving Charlie an antiseptic kiss on the top of his head, and stalked off. Charlie did not look up from Maggie's bag, which now had his undivided attention: there was a buckle that needed to be opened; on the other hand, resting on the floor, this bag made a splendid hobby horse.

Maggie collapsed on the floor beside Charlie. High above her the grown-ups—Signor T, Vicky, and Mike

—were holding a postmortem, which didn't interest her: her mission had been completed; Charlie was safe.

He was also surely about to bust bustable objects in her bag.

"Hey, you silly boy, stop that."

Charlie thought that was funny and bounced harder.

"No!" Maggie scolded.

Charlie didn't find that funny. He scowled at Maggie. He also socked her. Hard.

"No!" Vicky scolded adoringly.

Charlie's face contorted, got set for a huge howl.

"No!" Mike grabbed Charlie and threw him into the air. Charlie gasped, then laughed.

Life was back to its old everyday self. Charlie was

just an ordinary baby—cute and pesty. No longer peculiar, fascinating, and kidnapped.

And, she, Maggie, was just—what?

Fingers ruffled her hair. "This girl's a heroine." Mike said. "The genuine article."

"She sure is," Vicky agreed, beaming at her.

But she didn't feel like one. Right now, she felt like a kid from Tilton, Iowa, who was a long way from home.

"This calls for a celebration. Back to *San Marco?*" Mike asked.

"Oh, lovely. And Charlie will have his first view of the Piazza," Vicky answered. "Won't that be wonderful?"

Grown-ups! Maggie thought. The world could come to an end and they would still have education and culture on their minds.

Signor T regretted that he could not join them. Pressure of important business. Before he left, he got Maggie to one side.

"Remember always to keep your eye on the nudge. Until we meet again—perhaps?"

They shook hands.

That night, Maggie opened her window wide to a particularly brilliant Venetian night. Then, she curled up on her bed with a fresh pad of paper and began to write:

Dear Jasper:

Guess what? Today, I made a fortune! I made *six thousand and five hundred lire!* Which is about ten whole dollars! And guess what? I made it *baby sitting! ! ! ! !* . . .